Joe
AND THE HALLOWEEN MYSTERY

Joe

AND THE HALLOWEEN MYSTERY

JOHN TEOFILO PADILLA JR.

Archway Publishing books may be ordered through booksellers or by contacting:

Archway Publishing
1663 Liberty Drive
Bloomington, IN 47403
www.archwaypublishing.com
1 (888) 242-5904

Because of the dynamic nature of the Internet, any web addresses or
links contained in this book may have changed since publication and
may no longer be valid. The views expressed in this work are solely those
of the author and do not necessarily reflect the views of the publisher,
and the publisher hereby disclaims any responsibility for them.

Any people depicted in stock imagery provided by Thinkstock are models,
and such images are being used for illustrative purposes only.
Certain stock imagery © Thinkstock.

ISBN: 978-1-4808-5490-1 (sc)
ISBN: 978-1-4808-5491-8 (e)

Library of Congress Control Number: 2017916791

Print information available on the last page.

Archway Publishing rev. date: 10/29/2017

CONTENTS

PROLOGUE

The mystery of Halloween began at early dusk on October 31 in the gloomy year of 666 BC. A bright star fell from the highest sky down into the dark abyss, flickering as it lost its brilliant light of righteousness.

Halloween is celebrated once every year. The ritual of Halloween continues for a few days after November 1, which is called Día de los Muertos, or Day of the Dead. These yearly rituals of Halloween and the Day of the Dead are connected, as anyone researching this topic thoroughly would find out.

Halloween's dark, evil spirit eventually spread throughout the world. The origin of Halloween occurred near a huge stone pyramid somewhere in Mexico that reaches toward the heavens, surrounded by human skulls and cempasuchil flowers. This traditional pyramid is connected to a ball court, on which Mesoamerican peoples known as the Aztec and the Maya, and South American peoples known as the Inca, played a ball game called Game of the Gods. The ball they used, made of solid rubber, was called *olli* in the ancient Nahuatl language. This rubber ball was about fifteen to twenty centimeters (six to eight inches) in diameter, slightly smaller than a human head.

The scene opens up with a huge orb of light at the top of the pyramid. The orb looks like one huge all-seeing eye that is looking down toward the bottom of the pyramid, where a ball game is in progress. This action-packed Game of the Gods has specific rules that allow you to use only your elbows, knees, hips, or head to make contact with the ball. A huge muscular man wearing the royal headdress of a leader is a captured prisoner, playing ball for his life against a handpicked athlete named Molech, who has the face and head of a horned owl. Molech flexes his abdominal muscles to bounce the ball off his hips, allowing it to bounce only once off the ground. Then he uses his knee to bounce the ball through a ring hoop high on the stone wall, scoring the winning goal.

"No!" screams the frightened, muscular man with the royal headdress. He does not lose graciously, struggling when he is subdued instantly by four strong warriors. He is slowly escorted against his will up the pyramid steps toward an altar, where five priests of the highest rank await. The man, the chief leader of another tribe, is a prisoner. He resists with every step he takes, but he is overpowered nonetheless.

As they reach the top altar, the strong warriors slam their captive on the sacrificial stone. The five priests assume control by grabbing and stretching out his legs and arms. As the shirtless captive muscular man is being held down by the five priests, they force his back against the sacrificial stone in a way that exposes his chest for the purposes of a ritual sacrifice on the best night of the year—Halloween. The beat of the *huehuetl,* or vertical drum, begins. A musician beats on the drum, which is made of dried animal skin and mounted atop a wood frame, using two rubber-headed mallets to produce a two-tone note. The music is to please their feathered serpent god, whose mysterious past had him in charge of a divine orchestra of celestial music.

The fifth priest—a huge, muscular man named Saman—rises boldly to his feet—while the four other priest hold down

JOHN TEOFILO PADILLA JR.

their frightened captive. Big Saman wears ancient ceremonial robes made of fine plants with dried human skin and bones, and a face mask made of a human skull that's decorated with mosaics. He smirks...as he holds a smelly bloodstained knife over the man...who's forcefully being held down by his colleagues. The large crowd loudly cheers, "*Saman! Saman!*" The sweating man, nervously scared, lies helpless on the sacrificial altar...crying. His eyes frightfully open up more than normal—like large melons—while he watches the sharp knife aimed at his chest.

Saman smiles, exposing his funny-looking ugly teeth through the skull face mask. With no remorse, he strikes the helpless muscular man in the chest. Blood explodes out, bursting in the air like a fountain. Saman quickly reaches inside the man's chest cavity, pulls out the beating heart with his strong hands, and shouts in jubilation, "*Feliz cumpleaños, Satan!*" The ground and pyramid rumble, and then fire and smoke come out from the ground, forming smoky fire around Saman. Devilishly pleased, Saman hands the moving, loudly beating human heart to a demonic-looking feathered serpent dragon beast, who mysteriously appeared from the smoke.

The feathered serpent's brilliant emerald eyes hint that he was once possibly very beautiful, but he has since has fallen into this hideous demonic form. The feathered serpent—called *Kukulkan* to the Maya, *Quetzalcoatl* to the Aztecs, and *Supay* to the Incas—uses his strong hand to firmly hold a solid gold cup that has a human skull design on it. With his other hand, he positions the beating heart above the gold cup. He squeezes the beating heart to make the blood drop out into his gold cup, but some blood drips onto the cup's skull design. The feathered serpent puts the solid gold skull cup to his lips and smells the blood's aroma. His eyes show pleasure while he drinks the warm blood slowly. Then he proclaims, "This is the day I was reborn!

The hell I ween! This is my birthday! All I ever wanted was recognition…my honor, Father! I was forgotten! I had my pride! I still have my pride! I'll get my throne! One day I'll have a Novus Ordo Seclorum—New World Order!" His beast-like, evil-looking emerald eyes glow on Halloween night.

CHAPTER 1

Many thousands of years have since passed. The story moves on to the present century. A man named Joe is asleep in a huge bedroom of his inherited Beverly Hills mansion. He hears in his dream a song similar to the Eagles' song "Hotel California." He remembers the fierce battle he had with Satan, piercing the Devil with the archangel Michael's sword, plunging it deep into his chest, as he hears the song blast, "You just can't kill the beast." Then Joe sees a lake of flames and a huge snake with one large eye. The snake looks at Joe while it hisses angrily and slithers out of the lake. Joe suddenly wakes up from his nightmare.

Worried about what he had just dreamed, and feeling sad and alone, Joe wishes to see the Father. He says, "I don't even have my friend Herbie to talk to anymore and give me advice." Joe gets out of his bed and walks a few feet. Seeking calm, he spots his inversion board contraption. He inserts his feet, lies on the board, and leans backward until he is inclined ninety degrees, hanging upside down like a bat in a cave. Joe takes deep breaths in and out as he lies vertically inclined. It makes him feel good when his back is stretched and his brain has plenty of blood to think. While Joe relaxes and stretches his spine, he looks at the altar in the far corner of his room that he'd made for worship to God. The beautiful altar is made of lava rocks, jade and ruby stones, and two tablets of turquoise with the Ten Commandments inscribed on them. Joe's bedroom, with its heavy fireproof door, is locked from the inside with advanced celestial locks that no one can penetrate—not even Satan himself.

Joe leans forward. The board he is lying on tilts and swivels to an upright position. He unlocks his feet, stands up smoothly from the board, and then walks gracefully away like a powerful lion over to his altar. Joe gets down on his knees and places his hands together to pray. He wishes to visit heaven and use the keys given to him by God to help him on his holy missions of honor. Joe begins to pray, "Our Father, who art in heaven—" He suddenly enters beautiful heaven with his entire human body and spirit as he envisions an orb of celestial light. He feels God's glowing peaceful presence.

"Joe, my son, what troubles you?"

"Lord Father, I feel alone. It seems I've lost many people I loved who were once with me among the living," Joe sobs. Suddenly, he sees Herbie, his old parrot friend, fly from God's brilliant light and perch on his left shoulder. Joe beams with delight while Herbie kisses him with his little black tongue. "Herbie, my old friend, I missed you!" Joe says.

The Lord God proclaims, "Joe, even though I granted you eternal life after your life on earth, you are still mortal and can die! Son, the Accuser knows this. Be careful, Joe."

"I do not fear death, Lord God. But ..." Joe sheds a few tears.

"I know what you think, Joe," says the Lord God. "Herbie will be with you to comfort you, providing you with peace and advice. Remember, you have your Father's guidance. You know, Joe, Herbie is with you temporarily until your time endeth on earth—whence the earth is no more."

"The end? What do you mean, Lord God, Father?"

"Be gone, Joe!" the Lord God commands.

And then Joe finds himself back on his knees next to his altar in his bedroom. The good thing is that Herbie is with Joe now. "Let's go eat, Joe. *Irk!*" Herbie says, slobbering on Joe with his little black parrot tongue kisses.

"It's good to have you back with me, Herbie." Joe smiles with praise to God. The days continue to pass.

It's early afternoon on October 31, a sunny, bright, and windy Halloween Day at a Beverly Hills, California, cemetery. At this cemetery there is a young man standing alone holding flowers. His name is Joe Benson. He smoothly uses his left hand to conceal his sword at his left side inside his *saya*, or scabbard, while he holds the flowers with his right hand. Joe is incognito with his sword underneath his custom-made stealth garment that is part of his royal knight battle armor, which he left at home. As he stands there, an abundance of very attractive flowers appealing to the eye in his right hand, he takes a deep breath of air. A small wind moves the flowers in his hand. He then, with tears in his eyes, kneels down in front of his family members' tombstones. The cemetery caretaker walks by holding a pitchfork. Joe now relaxes to sit in the *seiza* position, moving the tops of his feet to the ground and, with his buttocks, sitting on the backs of his heels. Joe remembers his sensei, Musashi, stressing proper *reiho* (etiquette). Joe's companion pet parrot Herbie rests on his left shoulder. Joe remembers his sensei saying, "Your heart is full of fertile seeds waiting to sprout. Just as a lotus flower springs from the mire to blossom splendidly, the interaction of the cosmic breath causes the flower of the spirit to bloom and bear fruit in this world." Joe knows the importance of his role as an angel of God's righteous light to fight against the dark evil forces. Joe pauses his thoughts and says aloud, "I miss you, family, being among the living." He places the flowers with the lovely aroma softly in front of four tombstones. "These nice flowers sure do smell good!" Joe says. Herbie jumps off Joe's shoulder, smells the flowers, and looks at Joe with parrot tears in his eyes. On one tombstone is etched, "Scientist, Biologist, Biochemist, Doctor Robert Benson, and beloved wife, Olivia Benson, a ballerina of the English Ballet Theatre." The second tombstone reads, "Five-Star United States Army General Arnold Benson, who was a loving husband, father, and grandfather. "Honoring thy country starts at home!" The etching on the third tombstone reads, "Mary Benson, loving wife, and mother of Robert Benson." The fourth tombstone says, "Mr. and Mrs. Adolfo Newton, stars of the English Ballet Theatre, beloved parents of Olivia Benson."

"Mother, Father, grandfathers, and grandmothers, I love and miss all of you in the living!" says Joe. He pauses, tears flowing from his eyes. Joe now reflects on memories of his father, Dr. Benson, carrying him on his shoulders as he drank fresh water from their well, while his mother, Olivia, walked with them, in her beautiful backyard garden filled with fruit trees, flowers, vegetables, and a brook with edible trout. He remembers visiting his father the doctor while he worked at the hospital, and watching a ballet performance of his mother the great ballerina. He sheds more tears as he remembers listening to his grandfather Adolfo talk about old England. As he looks at the general's tombstone, he cracks a fond smile brought on by a memory. He remembers camping in the rugged mountains; learning to navigate by using the sun, the moon, and the seven celestial stars; learning how to find water underground; learning how to eat roots and bark; learning how to snare wild game; and learning to fish with a vine, using an insect as bait. But most importantly, he remembers listening to the benevolent guiding words of his grandfather the general, who often read the Holy Scriptures—the Word of God—by the campfire at night. Joe feels loss and sorrow while at his family members' tombstones. He positions himself to get more comfortable, using his well-developed leg muscles to sit in a samurai *Iaido* half-seated position.

Joe has a powerful divine sword, and is always at the ready for whatever may come, given that he never lets his guard down. Joe's powerful left hand grips his saya. Placing his controlling thumb over his *tsuka* (sword guard), he is ready to pull out his sword quickly with either hand. He remembers practicing this ancient authentic samurai lesson with the late Sensei Musashi. Joe, now focusing and breathing air in deeply, begins closing his eyes, remembering the time he was unable to see Sensei Musashi creeping up behind him, as if to launch a surprise attack on him. He remembers practicing this drill many times with his sensei, and fighting against evildoers who attempted to kill Joe. Joe was alerted to the presence of evildoers many times using his enhanced keen sixth sense. He remembers fondly that Sensei Musashi was indeed behind him that time. Joe reflects what happened when Sensei Musashi attempted to carry out a deadly surprise attack with his razor-sharp katana. Joe remembers instinctively using an Iaido draw to pull out his katana in time, raising it over his head to masterfully block and deflect Sensei Musashi's swing at Joe's back head.

Joe allows his mind to drift, recalling his Olympics fencing teacher Napoleon, from France, battling their swords' lines of defense. He also remembers listening to his grandfather the general speaking, and guiding him with words of benevolence. And somewhere in all his memories, he hears heart-inspiring music from his sister, Rose, who plays a finely tuned grand piano.

Joe now turns his thought to his life in the now. Sometimes he feels lonely, but his life has meaning and he is guided by a purpose. Joe knows he is a human who can be killed at any time. However, he has been chosen by the Father to be an angel, or a good deed messenger, while among the living here on earth.

He was blessed with extraordinary human powers from God to fight evil here on earth, and he was given a sword from heaven inscribed with "Archangel of Honor." Almighty God made it and gave it to him. Joe knows humans on earth are here for a reason, as God intended when he created humankind in his image.

When Lucifer was a grand cherubim, entrusted with many duties in heaven, Lucifer went along with God's plan, until sin was found in his heart. Lucifer desired his own throne like the Most High. Although he had access to all the places in heaven, he could not see the forest for the trees. Therefore, a battle in heaven ensued. Ultimately, Lucifer was transformed into the Devil—Satan, the Dragon—and was cast out of heaven, taking with him a third of the angels, whom he'd beguiled into believing in him.

Joe takes a deep breath to calm himself while bringing more oxygen into his bloodstream to muster up some energy. "Lord God, I know Satan wants to kill me, or have his demons do me in. I fear that if I have my own family someday, they will be persecuted by evil. However, now that I'm looking at my parents' and grandparents' graves, I've reconsidered. I have now been reassured within myself, knowing my parents and grandparents neither deterred their greatness nor feared evil. Consequently, they did form families out of love, and their love endured and was a thing of beauty in this world. Yes, it is a beautiful world if you look at the good things and not at the bad, evil things. Maybe this is why Lucifer first stumbled, and why he continues to stumble in his dark, evil ways," Joe says.

Joe's sixth sense feels danger. Suddenly, a cold wind blows a crying woman's message into Joe's ears. The chilling wind seems to say, "Ay, mis hijos!" (Woe, my children!) Just then, Joe, using his peripheral vision, turns his head around and spots a woman wearing a black funeral dress. With a black veil covering her face, she is moving without making a sound, observing Joe. This dark shadow is near a newly made cement statue of a woman crying. The lurking shadow appears to be waiting for Joe to let his guard down. Joe feels this.

Joe's memory flashes back to a lesson from his sensei, Musashi. The sensei had said, "Fear robs you of *heijoshin*—peace of mind. As a true samurai, Joe, you do not fear death, so why should you fear anything that life might throw your way?"

This mysterious woman seems to be mysteriously floating around the cemetery, crying with sounds of dark remorse. Joe cuddles his parrot Herbie. Herbie whispers, "Don't fear, Joe. The Father is with us. Awk!" Then suddenly the woman disappears. The wind continues to whistle.

Joe says, "Father, I know my days are numbered, being a human of flesh, blood, and bone, but Lord God, dear Father, nothing will deter me from my mission here on earth to do your bidding. I will love life and form a family someday. *Si Dios quiere!* God willing!" Still seated in a formal position, Joe is suddenly attacked from the rear by the cemetery caretaker, wielding his pitchfork. Immediately, Joe does an *ushiro*, drawing out his sword, and smoothly rear-thrusts it into the caretaker's body, using a technique called *suriyoku*.

"*Uhgh!*" screams the caretaker.

Spinning around with one fluid movement to face his opponent, Joe raises his sword overhead, intending to use the *monouchi*, the strongest and sharpest edge of the blade. He drops his sword downward vertically—*suichoku*. The sword makes a whistling sound—*whiff!*—cutting the caretaker's head—his *atama*—in half. *Splunk!* Joe then rises to his feet and flicks the caretaker's blood off his sword and onto the ground, performing the act of *chiburi*. Joe stands ready in the en garde position.

"Let's go home, Herbie," Joe says.

Herbie jubilantly flaps his parrot wings to take his position on Joe's left shoulder. He says, "Irk! Anywhere away from here, Joe!" Herbie then kisses Joe on the face with his black parrot tongue.

Suddenly, the woman statue comes alive, as if it has a demon inside it. The statue attacks Joe by swinging its hands. Joe bobs and weaves, slips, and backs away, like a boxer untouched. He attacks landing a forward smooth side kick on the statue's body, but he only knocks the heavy statue back a few feet.

Herbie flies off Joe's shoulder. "Careful, Joe; ark!"

The statue woman comes forward. Joe says, "I am man! Be gone, demon!" As the statue woman lunges at Joe, he sees that it has tears of blood. Joe redirects the heavy statue by grabbing one of its arms and using its own energy to guide it into a tree. *Crack!* The cement woman appears to crack a little. "Hmm," Joe whispers. He was taught well by Sensei Musashi to use the surroundings to his advantage.

"Break, Joe! Break, Joe!" Herbie shouts. Joe unsheathes his sword and does a *kirioroshi*, a two-handed cut across the statue's body. *Pop!* It breaks more.

The woman statue screams, "Man will die!" It growls like a beast, once more coming after Joe.

Joe brings his sword high over his head. "I rebuke you, demon!" He takes a step forward for momentum and simultaneously, with speed and power, brings his angel's sword downward, striking the statue's head. *Crack!*

The woman statue growls with sounds from hell. "You are nothing without the sword!"

Joe looks up to the heavens. "Father, why do they tempt you?"

Herbie shouts from the air, "Show them, Joe. Irk!"

Joe calmly sheathes his powerful sword from heaven. The demon inside the statue begins salivating blood from its mouth. Then it moves in Joe's direction. Joe sinks his body downward for a powerful balanced stance to draw ki energy from inside him. Then he lets loose with a right-hand palm strike to the center of the statue's body. *"Kia!"* Joe shouts, his body, mind, and spirit connected as one. *Kaboom!* The woman statue explodes into little pieces, crumbling to the ground, leaving cement dust in the air.

"Joe … Joe!" Herbie says, perching again on Joe's right shoulder.

"Let's go home, Herbie."

"What Joe say." Herbie kisses Joe with his little black parrot tongue. They leave the cemetery slowly, not nearly fast enough for Herbie. "Run, Joe!"

CHAPTER 2

A few hours later, in another part of the world, Tulum, Mexico, it's a baking hot sunny Halloween afternoon. In the city of Tulum the air is filled with foul-smelling cempasuchil flowers, which bloom by a gloomy castle called El Castillo, which is situated on the beautiful coast of the Gulf of Mexico. Inside El Castillo one can see and hear thousands of spiders running on the floors and walls. It seems one can hear their spider voices speaking of the desire for human flesh to bite. Yes, there inside El Castillo there is a gathering of many witches and warlocks, conversing while they stand next to many human skeleton skulls that are inside a *tzompantli* (skull rack), preventing spiders from attempting to climb them. There is also a black cat, purring and rubbing itself against the skull rack. These powerful witches and warlocks arrived here from all over the world to fuse their power together for a spectacular evil Halloween night. "Sit down. Welcome to my castle!" the powerful witch from Endor, whose name is Samara, evilly says. She proudly wears her black velvet gown.

There are spiders crawling all over the chairs, tables, and floors. The witches and warlocks flick them off their chairs with their hats or their hands. There are the screeching sounds of mice as they run rampant through the castle. Some mice run over some of the witches' feet. "Ahh!" the witches scream. When the witches look to the ceiling, they see many bats with large teeth hanging upside down. One bat comes down, flying into the neck of a warlock. Its teeth almost bite the warlock's neck, yet they do not, because the warlock grabs the bat, places it on the table in front of him, bite's the bat's neck, and then throws the creature on the floor, dead. "Let's get on with this meeting, Samara!" the warlock shouts.

Samara has a presence that is noticed by all. When she glares at you, her lure is attractive, but you sense a danger about her. The feeling of Halloween consumes Samara to desire extra energy. She goes into a trance, looking at her black cat. "Come here, my precious Jezebel!" Samara says. The familiar black cat jumps into Samara's arms. Jezebel growls like a small demon, with pus and saliva profusely spurting out of its mouth. Samara feels a sudden surge of evil, making her big, dark, puffy owl- and shark-like eyes open wide. She looks deep into her hypnotizing crystal ball, which is on the heavy table in front of her, as she relays her thoughts out loud. "Men are the reason the world will always have wars. Men are in positions of leadership over the world, but I want to change this. In my façade of a life, I am just a Mother Superior, not the pope, but with my knowledge, I should be the papa, not the mama. Men in this world discriminate, just as the fallen angel has told me. After all, no fallen angel would dare lie to me. I am Samara, the greatest witch ever!" Samara proclaims.

One of the warlocks stands. "Rubbish! I am a man! Men are not the problem in this world. Perhaps the women are. I feel offended, Samara! Take those words back, you *bitch* witch of a woman!" he says.

"I thought you might be the warlock who challenges me, but I wasn't sure—until now!" Samara raises one eyebrow. Giving a half smile, she continues. "I apologize to you, Warlock Chill, at this moment in time."

"Now that's better, Witch of the Dark!" Warlock Chill says, boldly sitting back down.

Samara suddenly spots something in her crystal ball. "Aha! Now I see a young man without his shirt on. He looks extremely athletic, with his muscles glistening. A healthy-looking parrot rests on his left shoulder. He is walking around some exotic garden. The sun shines on both of them. It must be a warm climate, probably somewhere in California. My witch powers read the young man's lips, saying, 'It felt good to visit my family at the cemetery, remembering them as they were among the living. Jesus will return in humankind's final days, but are we not there, yet?'" Samara now sees the young man pause, look over his shoulder, and say, "Hmm. Herbie, my sixth sense feel as if some dark force is observing me now!"

Samara also reads the parrot's lips, saying, "Joe! Feel ugly force, ugly face too. Yuk! Chirp!"

Samara says, "I cannot locate this exact area, and I don't like that bird, but I know now! This young man is called Joe. I feel his spirit, powerful, pure, and filled with goodness—aaauuh!" Samara's eyes become flooded with extreme pain; desperately she palms her burning eyes. "Rrruuh!" Samara cries, no longer able to look at the image of the young man named Joe.

"Samara, are you all right? Who was the young man you saw in your crystal ball?" one among the curious witches and warlocks inquires fearfully. Samara, in pain, ignores the question. She quickly plunges her burning eyes into a face bowl filled with softened wet *Camellia sinensis* leaves, which soothe her eyes. She remains quiet.

After a few moments, Samara lifts her face out of the face bowl and then dries her eyes with a Vatican towel she had confiscated. Samara takes a deep breath to calm her nerves, wondering silently whose power intervened and kept her from monitoring Joe on her witch's crystal ball. "Let's concentrate to fill our hearts with evil thoughts as we approach Satan's birthday on Halloween night!" Samara says.

A slithery Chinese witch named Chinara gives Samara an ancient Chinese herb that can be taken in liquid form.

"What reactions to consuming this herb will a person have?" Samara says.

"It will produce hydrocephalus, swelling and water on the brain, Samara. This is an ancient Chinese way of silencing some-one. Not all Chinese are privy to the properties of this herb," Chinara says. Samara is pleased by what she had heard. Her eyes opened up with delight as she used her long ugly fingers to quickly grab a small rodent that ran across the meeting ta-ble. She placed the rodent's head in her mouth and then bites it off— *pop!*—making a sound like biting into an apple. Then she consumed the rest of the rodent, which pleased her taste buds. Afterward, she licked her fingers.

The witch from London displays a grotesque facial expres-sion while observing Samara eat the rodent. "What are you going to bloody do with the herb, Samara?" Londonra whispers fearfully.

"It's for anybody who stands in my way!" Samara exclaims. She turns to another witch. "Romanra, you will be in Italy soon?"

"Yes, Samara," the witch from Rome, Italy, replies.

All the witches are in a curious state of mind, but none more than the very intelligent witch from Japan called Japanra. "I can feel you looking deep into my mind, Japanra. Stop it!" Samara says. Turning to the whole group, she says, "My exquisite witches and warlocks of power, we have come together for a mastermind meeting. Together we are stronger, especially on Halloween night." Samara lets loose a heart-pounding, skin-peeling, sadistically devilish laugh from hell.

Suddenly, a hissing noise can be heard next to Warlock Chill. The warlock has his legs open as he sits without *knickers*. The snake appears with devilish eyes, and opens its fanged mouth to bite the warlock in his exposed testicles. But the battle-ready warlock intercepts by putting his ancient wand into the mouth of the snake. The snake blows up like a balloon. *Boom!* Then Warlock Chill, using his right hand, puts his wand to his lips and blows air on it like a smoking gun. Warlock Chill says, "Another notch on my wand … cheerio!"

All the witches and warlocks climb the steep interior spiral staircase. Bats fly and shriek with their mouths open…as they bite several struggling witches on the neck…they climb to the rooftop of the castle. Once at the top, everyone who ascended the spiral staircase observes a small table with a mysterious glass of unknown liquid sitting there. A huge albatross lands on the corner of the rooftop. "What is that ugly bird of doom doing here?" Warlock Chill says. The albatross is stereotyped as the bird of doom.

Samara somehow seems to have a connection with the bird. The two look into each other's eyes, relaying messages. "Power, money, and sex are what the world desires most, but power is strength!" Samara says. Enthusiastically, Samara reaches for the glass and attempts to drink it, but she is halted by Warlock Chill.

"What is this drink for? And why you, Samara?" Chill asks.

"It's for Halloween the chosen one, but why do you ask, Warlock Chill? Are you implying you are more chosen than I? You are a man without conformity," Samara says as she again reaches for the glass of liquid.

"Yes. I'm chosen, Samara! And you shall be my concubine!" Chill says. Feeling no apprehension, he intercepts Samara with brute force, and then quickly drinks the liquid down.

"Yes, Chill. You are chosen—chosen to die!" Samara jeers. Chill quickly falls to the ground, trembling as he holds his head, which is in enormous pain—pain ten times that of a migraine. Samara looks at everyone in the eyes to calm them, behaving as the leader she is. "Let's make a circle and join hands. We'll think together to form a mastermind!" Samara orders. "Now close your eyes, witches and warlocks. We now can have a true blending of the minds with conformity as we sacrifice uncooperative Warlock Chill on Satan's birthday this Halloween!" Samara proclaims. All witches and warlocks excitedly observe Warlock Chill's head as it swells to the size of a pumpkin, which in medical terms is edema. His body is stretched out at full length on the floor. In an apparent coma, he is dying as the cool ocean air blows, at dusk, at Samara's feet.

CHAPTER 3

It's also dusk in Beverly Hills, California, as Halloween night approaches. Joe had his mind cleansed while he meditated in the beautiful Benson Manor garden. "My mind feels fresh and ready to tackle Halloween night, little buddy."

"Me too, Joe. Meditate. Chirp!" Herbie bobs his relaxed parrot head. Joe now moves away from the garden, and walks with a swagger to the swimming pool area. He positions himself alongside the deep end of the swimming pool. Herbie is still totally relaxed on Joe's left shoulder, and in deep parrot meditation—or asleep Joe thinks.

"Geronimo!" Joe shouts, holding his sword while plunging feet-first into the deep water. *Splash!*

"Awk! Awk! Herbie can't swim!" The parrot springs off Joe's shoulder in order to fly to safety.

"Always practice your awareness, Herbie. 'Stay alert; stay alive,' my police officer friend Jesse always says," Joe advises. Suddenly Joe, with only his head above water, gets a phone call on his poolside wireless red box phone. The caller ID indicates that the call is from Saman Industries. Herbie uses his parrot feet to push the button to turn on the red glowing phone's loudspeaker, so Joe can listen and talk.

The caller says, "Joe, be careful! This is Noah. There are evil spirit winds on Halloween night." Noah is a Chiricahua Apache Native American, and Joe's friend.

"Hello, Noah! You too be careful, my friend—from US Navy SEAL Team 6!"

Then Noah suddenly shouts "Geronimo!" as he jumps out of a military plane on Halloween night. Noah shouts "Geronimo!" not just because of military tradition but also to honor one of his ancestors, his great-grandfather Geronimo.

Joe thinks about what his friend just said. Then Joe says, "Hey, Noah! Are you still there? It sounds like you're doing a HALO exercise again in heaven's sky, jumping out of a perfectly good airplane."

"You're right, Joe. But remember, not everyone on the earth's ground will go up to heaven. They must have faith in Usen," Noah says. (Usen is the name Native Americans use for the one true God—as in the first commandment, "There is only one God.")

"Yeah, okay. Okay, Noah. You sometimes give me a lot of consternation, my friend!" Joe says, kidding with his friend over the phone. Joe now gets serious and says, "I am honored to have you as a friend, Noah. I know your great-grandfather Geronimo was one of the first Americans to understand that nature and God are connected."

Noah becomes silent for a few seconds. Falling through fluffy clouds, he adjusts the gas mask on his face, ensuring a good seal. Noah is on an exercise mission, with high-tech drones assisting. He is practicing martial law, which is something that the United States president can implement at any time by way of executive powers.

Noah finally says, "Joe, listen closely, my friend. I cannot talk long. These are the words of my great-grandfather Geronimo." Noah quotes Geronimo: "'I cannot think that we are useless, or

God would not have created us. There is one God looking down on us all. We are all the children of one God. The sun, the darkness, the winds, are all listening to what we have to say. When I was a child, my mother taught me to kneel and pray to Usen for strength, health, wisdom, and protection. Sometimes we prayed in silence; sometimes each one prayed aloud; sometimes an aged person prayed for all of us, and to Usen.'"

Joe smiles. "Amen." Knowing that Noah took precious time to inspire him, Joe says, "Good-bye, Noah! Thanks, and be careful, my friend!"

"Good-bye, Joe. And you be careful too, Joe, on Halloween night!" Noah says.

Joe places the house phone's receiver back on the cradle, hanging it up. Then he walks into the deep end of the pool, with only his neck and head above water. There he practices drawing his sword, thrusting his sword, slashing his sword, and using fast footwork, as his feet move forward against the water to advance against an imaginary powerful opponent. He feels the water's resistance against him. Joe, in the deep water up to his neck, practices quick reflexes and unsheathes his sword with his right hand, using *uke nagashi* to block or parry an imaginary opponent's sword. All the muscles of Joe's body, including those in his arms and legs, strain as Joe remembers Sensei Musashi teaching him this ancient samurai technique of being one with water, which is nature's way of building up the body's muscles, so the samurai can be ready for whatever may come.

As night falls, Joe says, "Okay, Herbie, it's time. We need to begin doing our rounds on this Halloween night." Joe gets out of his swimming pool and dries off with his towel while Herbie soars around, keeping a protective eye on his master.

A few blocks away from Joe's house, a group of children dressed up in skeleton costumes, accompanied by their parents, ring a neighbor's doorbell. A young man holding a luminously glowing red lantern opens the door. The children say, "Trick or treat!"

"Well. Well, hell … I guess we have skeletons at our door. What should I do? Oh yes, I know—pay the price for my safety!" Jack says with a sad face. Jack gives the children slightly wet red apples for them to place inside their trick-or-treat bags. The children, in their skeleton costumes, inspect their clean wet apples while they walk away from the house. Jack closes the front door, laughing. One of the children says in a loud voice, "Hey, Mom! Dad! My wet apple has teeth marks on it!" Jack, with a mischievous grin on his face, places his red glowing lantern on the floor next to him. Then, with no remorse for his actions, he begins to watch young men and women in the house bobbing for apples. Loud rock and roll music is being played inside the darkened house. Suddenly, the music is turned down. An old prune-faced man with one leg leans on his wood peg. Dressed like a pirate, he begins telling a story of a powerful rich magnate who is controlling Halloween's booming business.

One of the young men looks outside one of the windows and says, "Hey, Jack, it sure looks dark outside. Kind of spooky, huh? Let me borrow your red lantern, bro!"

Jack quickly grabs his red lantern. "No! Don't touch! But you can look at it." Jack conceals his motive as to why he had brought his red lantern to the Halloween party. He turns the lantern's knob higher to increase the strength of the glowing light, which hypnotically attracts people to glare at its aura.

Jack, ignoring everyone, finds his memory flashing back to the past, when he was a child. He remembers when his father gave him the red lantern to go fishing with his grandfather. He thinks about his proud Celtic Irish heritage. His father, Timothy O'Lantern Junior, said to him, "Here you go, my son. I love you, Jack!"

"Thank you, Father, but I don't know how to use a lantern. Can I have a flashlight just in case?" Jack said, pondering what to do.

Just then, Jack's grandfather arrived. "I'll teach you, lad! We'll go camping and fishing. I'll show you how we used ye ole red lanterns back in ye ole Ireland, my boy," Jack's grandfather Timothy O'Lantern Senior said.

Jack had kept his red lantern since the time he was a child, wanting to hold on to the gift from his father, Timothy O'Lantern Junior, many years ago.

When Jack went fishing and camping on Halloween night with his grandfather Timothy O'Lantern Senior, he stepped just a short distance away from the camp, taking his red lantern with him, to urinate by some trees. Once he'd turned the lantern's flame down for privacy, he heard a group of people walking into camp, where his grandfather was sleeping. Keeping his red lantern off, he crept toward the camp, hiding in the woods. He was traumatized when he saw a devil cult torture his grandfather to death. The members of devil cult mentioned that the old man had a child with him named Jack, having learned this from an informant who'd seen them both fishing earlier, and said they wanted to sacrifice the boy on Halloween night. The old grandfather, a proud, strong Irishman, claimed he was alone, until his last breath.

Young Jack's heart was pounding. His mind was traumatized as tears flowed profusely from his eyes. Trembling, he stealthily walked away from the area. He learned how to turn his lantern off and on quickly as he walked through the forest. He was very frightened, hyperventilating. There he was, a child with no mother and a drunken father. Except for his grandfather, Jack had no role models. In desperation, Jack asked for Satan's help to show him the way out of the forest. At that moment on

Halloween night, a demonic angel with half-handsome, half-beastly facial features appeared, horrifying Jack and blocking his path.

Jack cried, "Who are you? What are you?"

The half angel, half beast said, "You know who I am! You called me for a deal ..."

"I don't need any help. ... Please go away!" Jack cried, feeling dread.

The devil cult group loomed near, walking with lit torches in their hands. They muttered, "Little boy, little boy, where are you?"

A crooked smile came across the face of the half angel, half beast. "Say my name!" the angel beast said.

"Devil, Beast, Satan, please help, er, save me!" Jack pleaded, gulping.

"We now have a pact agreement, but saved? Ha-ha-ha! Well, you'll see! Everyone will die someday!" Satan said. He placed a never-extinguishing ember inside Jack's red lantern, and then pointed in the direction that Jack should walk. Jack's lantern had a bright red hypnotizing glow. He eventually found his way through the cold forest, comforted by his glowing red lantern, and located the road leading to his father's house.

Jack had never known his mother; she died giving birth to him. Jack's father, Timothy O'Lantern Junior, was often drunk, although he taught his only son, Jack O'Lantern, all he could. Jack grew up traumatized from having witnessed his grandfather tortured to death. He saw various psychologists through the years. On the tearful day when his father died of liver cirrhosis, he took comfort in holding his glowing red lantern.

These were the things Jack reflected on when thinking of his childhood, many years ago. Who knows how old Jack really is?

Jack's big eyes are hypnotically trained on his glowing red

lantern, as if he is receiving a message from hell on Halloween night. A female who is watching Jack snaps him out of his trance. "Jack, your face looks of evil demon possession. Snap out of it! You have my life in your hands, handsome. Use a flashlight."

Jack devilishly smiles and says, "I like fire better!" He then signals for some of his party friends to come with him. The group of young couples, wearing witch and devil costumes, walk out of the house. Jack escorts them with his glowing red lantern. The group of young couples are laughing as they get into Jack's fire-red-colored Ford Mustang Boss 302 with glowing red-spoke rims. A male passenger in the backseat says to the driver, Jack, "Hey, Jack, with your lantern, fire it up, devil boy!"

A female passenger with an alluring voice says, "Yes, Jack! Please fire it up, baby. Pass the booze, and maybe I'll reward you later with some sex. It's Satan's birthday. Anything goes! Let's party!"

Titillated by the moment, Jack lights up several marijuana cigarettes, opens up three liter-size bottles of Irish whiskey, and passes them out after first taking some big gulps of the strong whiskey himself. Jack, holding one whiskey bottle between his legs, can't control himself any longer. He takes a deep puff of marijuana, making the tip of the joint glow Halloween red. He loudly proclaims, "On Hell-o-Ween night, I am the original Jack O'Lantern, and I do whatever the *hell* I want! There are no rules or laws for me!"

Several passengers say, "Jack, you do this all the time."

"The Devil is going to claim you someday, Jack-ass!" says one of the young men in Jack's car, cuddling a big bag of potatoes.

Jack says, "I feel something watching me." He drinks down a couple more gulps of Irish whiskey. *"Burp!"* Then he turns the ignition of his tricked-out automobile and revs the powerful engine of his Ford Mustang Boss 302 muscle car. Alarmed, Jack spots a young man walking across the street in the dark, with a parrot on his left shoulder that has been observing him. The look on Jack's face shows fright as the young man with the parrot walks up to him.

"Hello! My name is Joe. I know who you are, Jack! Everyone has *free will* to choose."

Herbie shouts, "Free will—awk!"

Joe turns his attention to the young people in Jack's car. "Snap out of your trance. Listen up, folks. Please get out of the car, everyone—now! He's been drinking way too much to drive, or even walk, home," Joe says.

"Yeah, he's a devil! Get out! Awk!" Herbie shouts.

One person among the young group of couples replies, "*Fuck* you, goody-two-shoes boy, and you too, birdbrain!"

Jack, devilishly grinning, thinks, *I win.* He takes more gulps of whiskey, and then he throws the half-filled bottle at Joe.

Joe smoothly lets the fast-flying bottle go over his right shoulder. He remains untouched, like a professional boxer. *Crack!* The bottle breaks on the sidewalk. Jack's dark, evil eyes—looked like those of a shark—glared with fury at Joe. Then Jack pushed the car door open fast… trying to hit Joe. But Joe, using good footwork, retreats, something he had learned to do when training for the Olympic gold medal in fencing. Jack exits his vehicle and attacks Joe with a jackknife kick. This is followed by a heel kick with his other leg.

"*Damn* it!" Jack says, both kicks having missed Joe. Joe immediately kicks vertically and straight out with his front foot, landing a hit onto Jack's abdomen, knocking Jack back to land on the ground.

"No fancy-pansy, Jack!" Joe says.

"Irk! Pansy!" Herbie says.

Then, Jack's friends exit the vehicle, one wielding a crowbar and another holding a sack of potatoes. Herbie flies up over the man with the crowbar and drops warm poop onto his face. "Err." The man groans. Joe snatches his crowbar and throws it far away, into a shrub. Seeing Jack getting up, Joe quickly judo-flips the man with poop in his eyes into Jack, knocking them both to the ground.

The man holding a sack of potatoes throws a potato at Joe, but Joe slaps it away with his tough martial arts hands. "Here it comes, potato man!"

"These taters will stop you!" The man holds his potatoes against his chest to prepare for Joe's powerful side kick. Joe glides forward fast with good footwork, and smoothly launches a side kick. *Kapow!* The young man, now holding mashed potatoes, goes flying twenty feet into some trash cans. "I eat taters!" Joe says.

Jack pops open his switchblade and slashes at Joe's throat— *whiff!* He misses Joe by a hair. Jack's two friends scramble back to the car. The experienced Joe, adrenaline pumping, says, "Drop your knife, Jack!" Joe unsheathes his sword.

"Hey, man, he's got a sword, Jack!" one of Jack's friends shouts.

Jack says, "I got something for you, *punk!*" Jack tosses his knife at Joe, and Joe parries the knife away in midflight. It falls to the ground. "This will fix you, parrot man!" Jack gets his glowing red lantern from his vehicle.

Herbie goes up high in the air. "Close eyes, Joe; eyes Joe," Herbie says.

Joe sees and feels a bright red burning light. He closes his eyes, places his holy sword in front of him in the center line vertical position, with the flat of the blade facing his opponent to shield his eyes and repel the dark evil force, and says a silent prayer: "Father, help me."

A bewildered Jack says, "Why is my red lantern not working on you?"

Instantly Joe, using his sixth sense and with his eyes closed, moves forward with good footwork, and strikes the red lantern with his sword. *Clank!* It falls to the ground.

"My lantern! You dented my lantern. Leave my lantern alone. Damn you!" Jack picks up his lantern and jumps back into his powerful muscle car, cradling his glowing red lantern.

Joe shouts, "Don't take them with you!"

"Why not? Everyone has a choice. ... I had a choice," Jack proclaims. Then he speeds away with his passengers.

One of them says, "Wowee! Pedal to the metal, Jack! This car is in mint condition. Do you have a connection with someone powerful? Where did you get this classic automobile? Hey, Jack, did you know that person with a parrot? Was he some kind of angel, because you sure are a devil, Jack!"

"Ha-ha-ha!" They all laugh. Jack ignores the questions, touching his red lantern while speeding down the road.

Everyone is smoking marijuana and drinking Irish whiskey. They start singing a Halloween song about devils, witches, and ghouls. Then, as Jack drives around a bend in the road, a fast-moving police squad car's lights come on. The police car is behind them, almost on Jack's bumper. A loud voice comes over the public-address speaker, saying, "This is Officer Jesse. Please pull over and stop your vehicle." Jack just grins and keeps going. Suddenly, the police car blasts its sirens. *Woo-err!*

The patrol car continues its pursuit as Jack shouts abusive profanities. He sees a bend in the road. Then the road becomes a straightaway. Jack says, "Okay, fuzz pig, it's time to open her up." He reaches below the dashboard, where a small tank of NOS—nitrous oxide—he'd deviously installed is mounted. Jack flicks on the metal switch, releasing the nitrous oxide, which sends instant power to the already powerful Ford Mustang Boss 302. *Boom!* Conniving Jack, using technology to gain an advantage, bursts down the road, his car like a dragster, leaving the police car miles away, and out of sight. "Yeah, baby!" Jack says.

Suddenly, an ugly deformed nude male midget carrying a pumpkin runs across the road in front of Jack's car. "Yuck! What the hell is that gruesome thing?" Jack's passengers scream.

Jack smiles, enjoying this Halloween moment. As he witnesses his passengers screaming, he feels an extra high in his bloodstream, which is filled with a potent mix of hard liquor and marijuana. Now he wants some kind of thrill. He shouts, "I'm a Celtic Irishman!" as he continues to speed on Halloween night.

The nude male midget runs again in front of Jack's car, but this time he throws his pumpkin, which is glowing with candlelight, at Jack's front window. *Splat!* The nude deformed midget shouts, "Satan's birthday!"

Jack tries to hit the evil-looking midget, but he fails to do so. He turns on his windshield wipers to clear away some of the pumpkin that's burning with fire. One of Jack's passenger's cries, *"Hell!* This car feels like hell on wheels!" Jack attempts to maintain control of his car, but he does as a curious cat does. He takes his eyes off the road, looking at the gruesome midget, and in bewilderment says, "What the *hell* is that?"

Everyone in the car screams in fear, "Jack! Look out!"

Jack quickly focuses his blurry vision back on the road in front of him, but it's too late. He drives off the road. The car caroms into the air and begins dropping down a deep canyon. As the car is in the air, Jack's heart beats strong. The smell of death surrounds him. His passengers scream, "Aaahh! *Help!*" Jack, feeling the thrill, nonchalantly looks out his driver's-side window. As his car, flaming with burning pumpkin, approaches impact, he suddenly sees the grim reaper, a skeletal figure in dark ropes, holding a staff and standing on the ground, looking up at him with an evil welcoming expression. Saddened, Jack attempts to feel comfort as he did when he was a child. He reaches for his glowing red lantern. Grabbing it, he holds it close to him. *Boom! Crash!* The powerful Ford Mustang Boss 302 explodes, killing all of Jack's young passengers on Halloween night. Jack, however, being cursed, is unharmed. He etches another notch on his endlessly glowing red lantern. Then he walks off into the woods, crying and carrying his glowing red lantern. Jack always regrets the Halloween when he'd made a pact with the Devil. But he made that choice of his own free will, just like the young adults who got into Jack O'Lantern's car on Halloween night.

JOHN TEOFILO PADILLA JR.

CHAPTER 4

On the same Halloween night, several young children from Joe's neighborhood, ages eight through twelve, are in a Beverly Hills, California, garage forming a music band. The children vigorously play their music on Halloween night, attempting to acquire good rhythm. Suddenly, out of frustration, one of the kids says, "We all suck to … *Hell!* I would give anything for us to play better! Anything!"

Suddenly, after that comment, a gruesome-looking baby with wings appears in front of them. One of the children shouts, "Hey, look! It's a cherub!" (A cherub is an angel that looks like a naked baby with wings.) However, some cherubs are not good, because some are fallen angels from heaven who followed the Accuser. The cherub plays devilishly beautiful music, using an unusual timbrel and musical pipe instruments. The children are in awe of this music played brilliantly by the small hideous-looking brownish-green creature with baby features. But even though they are fascinated by the music, they feel an aura of evil protruding from this creature.

"Do you know who I am on this Halloween night? If not, surely you feel who I am. I ask very little of you."

One boy says softly, "I'm afraid. … What do you want?"

"If you give me your heart and soul, and do what little I ask, then I will make you great musicians who play music everybody desires to hear! And you will be rich and famous for a short period of time, with your desires fulfilled and with the pleasures of this world within your grasp. I promise!" the cherub says, slurring. Drool from his mouth hits the floor. His eyes glow like a cat's in the dark.

The children don't feel right. Their hearts are pounding hard with fear, and their knees are buckling. Some lose their balance and fall to the ground. The children, horrified, begin quickly looking at each other. Then suddenly they run—although some crawl—away, seeking to quickly go into the house, screaming, "Mom! Dad!"

The cherub, devilishly desiring them, attempts to grab one of the children, but he misses. That young boy slips out of the garage with his younger brother, where he observes a young man with a parrot on his shoulder walking a short distance away. "Help me!" the boy shouts, pushing his younger brother out in front of him. Joe instantly knows what has happened. Suddenly, the little cherub springs from its hiding place in the garage to attack Joe. Joe immediately unsheathes his sword and uses a downward-slicing *nukitsuke* to slash-cut the cherub across his evil little ugly body, preventing him from completing the attack. Then Joe flicks his sword down to the ground to shake the blood off it, performing chiburi.

Instead of fighting, the cherub disappears to escape. Joe says, "Herbie, my sixth sense tells me something evil is still here."

Herbie stares at Joe and says, "You aren't crack-a-lacking, Joe. Hey, let's go back home, Joe. Awk!"

Suddenly two children run to Joe and say, "Please help us, mister!"

"Don't worry, children, I'll walk you home." Joe smoothly, like a samurai, completes a *noto*—the act of resheathing the sword into its *saya*. Then he calmly says, "Here! Use my royal phone to call your parents."

"Thanks, mister. ... Hey, aren't you the US Olympic fencing champion?" one of the boys asks.

"Well, yes, I am. It was good technique, good exercise, good nutrition, and a good pure knowledgeable mind with, most importantly, faith with all my heart—in God—that allowed me to win," Joe proudly says.

"I saw you on television fighting with your sword. You're totally awesome!" little Eddie says. Then he uses Joe's royal phone. "Hey, Dad, me and Mike are walking back home now with our neighbor Joe. He is the world fencing champion. Okay?" Eddie says.

"Okay, fine, Eddie. I know Joe, and I knew his father—good people. I'll be waiting for all of you. And let me speak to Joe, please," the father says. Joe conveys to the children their father's reassurance. They all begin walking.

Little Mike keeps looking at the sword Joe is wearing at his side. He says, "Hey, Joe! Are you wearing a real sword? It looks real. Or is it a fake, a replica?"

Eddie gawks at Mike. "Duh, it's Halloween night, stupid!"

"Settle down, children," says Joe.

"Settle down, children. Irk! Settle down. Awk!" Herbie says.

Mike and Eddie look at Herbie. Mike says, "That bird is a piece of work. No candy for you, birdbrain—only for Joe." Herbie takes off from Joe's shoulder and soars up high, flying around to keep a watchful eye.

Suddenly, a black cat runs across Mike, Eddie, and Joe's path. "Meow. Rrrr!" says the black cat.

Herbie swoops down and says, "You want a piece of me? Awk!" Herbie chases the cat away.

The two boys are in awe of the beautiful bird Herbie. "Maybe we should give him a little bit of candy?" Eddie says. The two boys offer the candy first to Joe.

"No, thank you. I eat only fruit."

Then they offer some candy to Herbie. Herbie is grateful. "Crunch! Swallow!" Herbie says, chowing down on some delicious candy.

"You're going to have to work those calories off, Herbie," says Joe.

"Gulp! I know Joe. I'm sorry, Joe. Awk!" Herbie says.

They walk several blocks. "Hey, boys, there's your father. Hello, Mr. Robinson!" Joe says.

"Hello, Joe! Thanks for walking my two boys home," Mr. Robinson says. "Would you like to come inside for a cup of joe?" Mr. Robinson asks.

"Yes, sir, Mr. Robinson. You own the famous organic coffee shop on Rodeo Drive. I've tasted your style of coffee. It's excellent. But I can only stay for a moment. I've got to go do my rounds—er, uh, walk. I need to keep in shape, you know!" Joe says. They all go inside Mr. Robinson's home on this Halloween night.

A few blocks away, Rose arrives at a house to help the neighbors with babysitting. She observes the rule of helping others. At the front of the house, Rose unlocks the padlock on the steel gate of the fence.

The widowed father had previously given Rose the key to the lock in case of emergency. Once Rose is inside the house, he says, "Hi, Rose."

"Hello, Mr. LaVaughn," Rose says. Information is mutually conveyed between Rose and Mr. LaVaughn.

Before Mr. LaVaughn departs to work a graveyard shift at the Saman Corporation, he kisses his two daughters, Amanda and Michelle. He says, "Before you go to sleep, say your prayers. Daddy loves you! Good night, little princesses!"

"Good night, Father. We will miss you," Amanda and Michelle say simultaneously.

Mr. LaVaughn regrets that his children no longer have a mother. The children's mother died from a heart attack after having seen something frightful on a previous Halloween night. The father says, "Please take care of my little girls, Rose. And please call me at my work if there are any emergencies. Most importantly, Rose, do not answer the door for anyone who is trick-or-treating."

"Please do not worry, sir. My brother, Joe, will swing by to check on us."

Mr. LaVaughn says, "I saw some witch on Halloween when I was child. She said her name was Samara. She looked as if she was possessed by an evil demon."

"Oh, how awful!" Rose says.

"I'd rather not talk anymore about Halloween nightmares, Miss Rose, but my memory of that witch called Samara is so real. Again, please do not answer the door to anyone, although the entrance gate is locked. No one can get in. Good-bye, Rose." The father takes out his key to the secured gate.

"Good-bye, sir, and don't worry," Rose says.

Once Mr. LaVaughn is gone, Rose checks in on the two girls, who are now in their bedroom, and then goes to the back family room, away from the noisy street out front, so she can read the Holy Bible. She just opens the Bible at random and begins reading the first page she sees. On this Halloween night, she reads the story about the fallen angel Molech who desires to acquire young children for sacrificing. This reminds Rose of an actual place called Bohemian Grove, a twenty-seven-hundred-acre private woodland camp located in Monte Rio, California. Bohemian Grove is where a huge statue of the horned owl Molech was created for making human sacrifices beneath it. Many humans who have somehow acquired power in this world attend there once every year, most of them on Halloween night.

As Rose reads, the two daughters, Michelle and Amanda, whose bedroom is in the front part of the house, fall fast asleep. Amanda is a peaceful heavy sleeper, whereas energetic Michelle is a light sleeper.

Suddenly, right before midnight on Halloween, while everyone in the house is asleep, Michelle awakens. It is an unusually hot Halloween night, with the wind whistling. Afraid, Michelle hears footsteps outside the front of her house. They sound like the steps of a huge person, probably a man wearing heavy dress shoes. Mysteriously, the heavy person starts walking up the passageway to the front door, seemingly without even having to have jumped or broken the tall locked gate—just walking as if he had walked through the gate. The little girl Michelle, trembling with fear, wonders what is going on. Suddenly the person's heavy footsteps stop at the front door. Michelle clutches her blankets. Then she hears the front screen door make loud screeching sounds, as if something with large cat claws is clawing at the screen door hard—a call to Michelle requesting to gain entrance.

Rose, at this moment, hears a woman crying in front of the house, saying, *"Ay, mis hijos!"* (Oh, my children!) Suddenly, Rose hears a light growl from either a lion or a dragon at the front door. Rose, trembling in fright, gets up from her chair, dropping her Bible and cell phone onto the floor. Hyperventilating and in a panic, she desperately looks for her cell phone but cannot find it. Then she nervously picks up the home's landline, placing the receiver it to her ear. As she attempts to call her brother, Joe, she hears a fiery inferno with many people crying in pain. A powerful evil voice says, "Open the door!" Rose drops the phone to the floor and places her hands over her mouth. She starts walking to the front door area with her hands over her mouth, trembling, attempting not to scream. Nevertheless, she screams her lungs out: *"Aaaaa!"*

The scream brings Michelle to scream, *"Aaaaa!"* She desperately wants to run to her babysitter Rose, or to wake her sister, the sound sleeper, who's on a single bed against the opposite wall, but she is too scared to move. Even though the hot weather, unusual for Halloween night, is unbearable, Michelle, crying heavily with fright, quickly puts her thick blanket over her face. This causes her to sweat even more.

Joe, having just left Mr. Robinson's house, is only a few houses away, walking with Herbie on his shoulder. Suddenly, they both hear women screaming. Joe quickly unsheathes his holy archangel sword of honor. He says, "Herbie! That voice sounds like Rose. My sixth sense feels evil near!" He runs toward Michelle's home, where Rose is babysitting. Herbie hangs on, grabbing the nape of Joe's neck, as if riding a horse at the Kentucky Derby.

Herbie says, "Go, Joe! Faster, Joe! Awk!"

At this moment, Michelle, crying hysterically and terribly frightened, shouts in her mind, *God help me!* Then the noise outside suddenly stops, and she feels peace. She falls back asleep as Joe confronts several demons outside her bedroom window.

"Don't worry, Joe, I've got your back! Irk!" Herbie bravely says. He springs off Joe's shoulder. His parrot eyes are wide open as he soars overhead and gives advice to Joe, who is about to engage in a fight with three demons. Joe attacks the demon at the front door. The other two are outside Michelle's window. Joe, with his sword in his right hand, extends his arm fully to command a powerful driving force with both legs, launching his entire being forward like a shot from a bullet, propelling him airborne. He is soaring, defying gravity. His sword thrusts through the demon's chest.

"Ahrr!" the demon cries, falling hard to the ground. *Thud!*

Joe, knowing that his sister is babysitting little Michelle and Amanda inside, shouts, "Hey, Rose! Is everything all right?"

Rose, still in shock, peeks out through the front living room curtains and sees her brother, Joe, confronted by two hideous creatures. *Devils?* Rose wonders. Then she runs to where the children are. Outside, Joe angles his sword to use the flat side of the blade, reflecting moonlight onto the two devils.

The devils, feeling Joe's powerful goodness, run away, growling, "*Hrr-loween!*"

Herbie shouts, "Joe! Joe!"

Joe smiles at his pet Herbie and then takes a breath. "Thank you, Lord!" He resheathes his sword and then knocks on the front door.

Rose opens up the front door and says, "I'm fine, Joe! Please come in." After hugging her brother, she goes to Michelle's and Amanda's bedroom and observes that both children are comfortably asleep and safe. She now goes to hug her brother.

Joe says, "It's okay, proud sister! You are strong. I will always be here for you, Rose!" Joe kisses his sister on her forehead to reassure her.

"Thank you, Joe!"

Herbie lofts in through the open door and says, "Man, it's dark outside. The moon … gone. We stay inside, Joe? Awk!"

Joe shakes his head no and then looks outside on this dark and gloomy Halloween night. The moon suddenly disappears, a dark cloud mysteriously covering it. He smiles at Herbie. Then he says, "Rose, you stay inside and secure everything." Rose kisses her brother on the cheek, giving him a warm sisterly hug. Joe smiles. He turns to depart with Herbie. He hears Rose securing the front door lock—*click!* "Herbie, we'll go home later. But on Halloween night, we need to keep patrolling this huge neighborhood—even if we have to stay out all night," Joe proclaims.

As Joe walks, with Herbie perched on his shoulder, a police car approaches slowly. Joe's excellent vision allows him to identify the police officer inside the car. He puts his thumb out to possibly get a ride.

"Hey, Joe, it's not safe to hitchhike. And I'm on duty, which means I shouldn't give anyone a ride. But you're not just anybody, Joe. You're also a reserve volunteer, an officer without pay—and brother, those are few to none!" Laughing, Police Officer Jesse says, "Need a lift, partner? Get in, Joe. ... And you can vouch for the bird, I assume?"

"Name's Herbie, you security guard. Irk!" Herbie says.

A bewildered Jesse says, "Well, doggies, the bird can talk. And he's a piece of work too."

"He is a celestial parrot and my friend, Herbie is," says Joe. His sixth sense tells him that Jesse is a good human being who was brought up with wholesome southern country values. "Thank you, Jesse! I'd appreciate the ride, partner. It's going to be a long Halloween night. Hey, Jesse, are you going by Mr. Robinson's organic coffee shop on Rodeo Drive?"

"Yup! You read my mind, Joe. I could use a good cup of joe. Everyone back at the precinct says tonight's not going to be some western movie, but some kind of horror picture. Go figure, Joe. That'll be the day when I see some monster. And *I ain't superstitious, Joe!* Do you read me, partner?" Jesse says.

"I read you, Jesse. And I approve of fresh ground coffee beans to make a cup of joe anytime," Joe says.

"Long Halloween night, Joe. Awk!" Herbie says, shaking his parrot head.

"I'm with you, pigeon bird friend," Jesse says.

"Parrot! Herbie a parrot. Herbie a knight! Be careful. Irk!" Herbie roughly says.

"Well, doggies! Now just cool down, my ruffled feathered friend. What's this knight thing?" Jesse, wondering, says.

"Oh, it's just Herbie. He's always kidding. Settle down, Herbie. Remember, a knight displays the characteristic of modesty," Joe says. Herbie nods his head in approval, and then eats the cracker Joe gives him.

After a few minutes, they arrive at the organic coffee shop on Rodeo Drive. Jesse smoothly swerves into the front parking spot designated for police. A wide smile appears on Jesse's face as he spots the lovely blonde struggling actress working inside. He says, "Amelia!" She works part time at the organic coffee shop, hoping that someone famous will pass through and see her potential for Hollywood.

Jesse and Joe step out of the police vehicle. Just before they go inside the coffee shop, a large group of motorcycles, about 666 in all, driven by men wearing white skeleton masks, stop outside the coffee shop. The leader, very tall, is wearing a white skeleton mask that flickers with red flame. The lead biker gets off his Harley-Davidson, walks toward Joe, and stands approximately two feet in front of him. While this is happening, Jesse places his hand on his firearm, ready to pull it out if needed. Joe looks directly at the leader and portrays heijoshin—a peaceful state of mind, righteousness. The leader of the motorcycle group quickly steps backward and shouts, *"Augh! I will see you again!"* Then he jumps on his bike and waves his followers forward. They all flee the scene. *Varoom!*

Jesse says, "What the hell was that about, Joe?"

"I do not know, Jesse. Let's go inside and get a cup of joe, buddy."

"Hello, Joe! Hello, Jesse! Hey, little Herbie!" Amelia says.

"Two cups of joe, please, Miss Amelia," Jesse says.

"Joe! Joe!" Herbie says as he grabs a bag of pistachios.

Joe smiles at Amelia and says, "Two bags of pistachios too, and please forgive me for Herbie's manners, Amelia. It's a long Halloween night, and Herbie's a little hungry."

"I forgive you and Herbie. After all, Herbie's hungry, right? And it's party time on Halloween. I sure would like to be escorted by you, Joe, to that new dance club called Club Saman later tonight," Amelia says.

Quickly, Jesse intercepts the moment. "Joe's engaged to a lovely girl who is the woman of his dreams, but I would be honored to escort you, Miss Amelia, right after I get off my shift, which won't be too much longer. But let's go somewhere like an Italian restaurant. Clubs just aren't safe, Miss Amelia, on Halloween night."

"You've got a date!" Amelia replies.

Joe and Jesse sit down to drink their cups of joe. Herbie eats pistachios. The three of them see children and adults alike dressed in Halloween costumes running by the coffee shop.

Some of the children come inside the coffee shop and shout, "Trick or treat?" Amelia kisses the children, and tosses chocolate bars inside their bags. Joe places a Benjamin Franklin inside Amelia's tip jar. Amelia graciously gives Joe a deep, sensuous kiss on his face, her lips touching the corner of his mouth. As Joe blushes, his sixth sense alerts him to something happening outside.

Jesse is radioed by police dispatch, the dispatcher informing him of an unknown assailant wearing a funny-looking Halloween mask who has just, for no apparent reason, knifed an old circus clown who was giving out candy on Rodeo Drive. "10-4! 1 Beverly-12, copy!" Jesse replies. From inside the organic coffee shop, he pushes his remote control to lower his police car's driver's-side window all the way down. "Got to roll, pilgrims! I'll see you shortly, Amelia!"

Jesse says. Amelia winks affectionately at Jesse, and Herbie winks his parrot eye affectionately at Amelia. "I'll take care of Amelia for you, Jesse. Awk!" Herbie says. Joe just sips his cup of joe, knowing that he has to roll soon, too, since its Halloween night.

Like a country boy, Jesse jumps into his police vehicle through the open driver's-side window, without opening the door. He turns on his police siren and then squeals his, burning rubber as he takes off down the road.

Amelia says, "Wow, that remote control window technology Officer Jesse just used, comes from Saman Industries. I heard the owner of Saman Industries is the one who opened the new dance club, Saman."

Just then, a huge nighttime security guard named Hamburger, a NFL player whose ethnicity is African American, walks into the café eating a sandwich. He says, "Happy Halloween, Ms. Amelia! May I have a cup of joe for the road to wash down my sandwich?"

"Sure, honey. And it's on the house. You know that you're our favorite security guard, handsome," Amelia says.

"Much obliged, ma'am! Good-bye, Miss Amelia. And if you need anything, please call me on my cell phone," Hamburger says. Hamburger leaves, sipping his coffee, and eating the sandwich he had brought from his baby momma's home.

Joe gets up and walks over to a bookshelf inside the café. Seeing plenty of quality books to read, he remembers his late father, Dr. Benson, saying to him, "Joe, read deeply from all books, but especially from the Good Book, the Holy Bible." Joe takes two books off the shelf, one called *History of the Coffee Bean* and the other being the Holy Bible. Joe reads quickly through the book *History of the Coffee Bean*. He sips on his cup of joe and begins reading Ephesians 6:11–12 from the Bible: "Put on the full armor of God, so that you can fight against the devil and his followers, against the rulers and authorities that have power from the dark force from the abyss."

Suddenly, Joe's sixth sense alerts him to something. The front door of the coffee ship swings wide open. A small, dark-clothed, dry- and scaly-skinned old man walks inside, limping on smelly gangrenous legs while holding a wooden walking stick—*cluck! cluck! cluck!*—that has a handle made of a real human shrunken head, which has decayed into a skull. "New Orleans is I from! May I have bit of java, please?" the man says in a Creole accent, leering devilishly at Joe.

Amelia says, "Coming right up, sir."

"Babalao is my name, girl," he says, smiling with gold and silver teeth. Then he continues to stare down Joe, attempting to intimidate him, but Joe remains calm. From his pocket, Babalao pulls out a voodoo doll that looks like Joe. He then inserts needles into the doll's head, arms, and legs, while chanting a curse. "I was sent from Papa Legba to guide you to the dark abyss. ... Fall ye down, man! In the name of Damballa, the great evil serpent spirit, fall ye down, man! Papa Legba demands it!" Babalao says.

Joe, laughing, says, "He's not my papa! Abyss? Maybe I should visit there one day ... to clean house!" Joe, not worried, continues to drink his cup of joe and read from the Good Book as if nothing has happened.

Amelia places a cup of coffee down on Mr. Babalao's table. He conceals the doll from her eyes. "Here you are, sir," Amelia says.

"Thank ye, girl. ... Oh, would you please give me a small lock of ye hair?"

Amelia is puzzled. "My hair?"

Joe steps in. "No, sir! Please do not partake in voodoo around here," Joe says. Herbie concurs, shaking his head no, while Babalao looks at his doll and then looks at Joe, stunned.

"You do not fall down, man, with the magic. Why? I, Babalao, decree you to die, man! Why you not fall?" Frustrated, Babalao quickly changes his voodoo attacks and spreads out his cards on the table. He flips one card that shows a gravesite in Haiti, and smiles. Suddenly, cracker residue falls from above onto Babalao's face and cards, causing the old man to cough. Babalao, coughing, looks up toward the ceiling. He sees Herbie high on a perch, eating crackers that are stacked in his talons. Many pieces fall onto Babalao's face.

Herbie laughs with *puff-puff* noises and says, "Awk! Careful?"

Babalao angrily swings his stick, with the sharpened teeth of the skull head facing Herbie. "Be gone, bird!" he says. Herbie flies away. Mr. Babalao, grimacing, shouts, "You're a marked man!" Then he swings the handle end of his walking stick and smashes Joe's coffee cup to pieces. He laughs as coffee splashes onto Joe, desecrating the Bible on Joe's table.

Amanda, holding Joe back, says, "Please leave, sir." Herbie, flapping his wings, ready for battle, looks at Joe, letting Joe know he is not alone.

Joe says, "You heard the lady. Please leave, sir."

Babalao spits on the floor in front of Joe. Then he chants, "Baka get you! Voodoo spells on Joe."

But Joe just smiles, remembering his sensei saying, "Joe, a true warrior contests with nothing. Defeat means to defeat the mind of contention that we harbor within."

Suddenly, an ugly beast of a dog comes up, opens the café's front door, and growls viciously at Joe. Babalao boldly says, "Yes, is Baka come to get you, man!" Baka is medium-sized with muscles like a pit bull but with the speed and hunting skills of a coyote. Babalao salivates as he holds his cane out to strike Joe. Joe unsheathes his sword and assumes the fencing en garde position. He breathes slowly, his adrenalin pumping, ready for whatever Halloween may bring him.

Herbie advises, "Two of them, Joe. Keep eye, awk!"

"Halloween night is mine, and you goes down, man!" Babalao says. He viciously swings his cane horizontally at Joe. Smoothly, Joe ducks under the cane. While still low, he extends his sword to pierce Babalao's right knee, and then fluidly moves his sword slightly right, slashing the charging beast dog with the teeth of a lion across its mouth, splashing blood into the air, sending its huge teeth everywhere, with some landing into coffee cups—*clink!* Joe, still on one knee, flicks his sword to the ground to symbolically remove the opponent's blood, thereby completing the chiburi.

In extreme pain, Babalao shouts, "You will get yours, man!" He and the beast dog exit the coffee shop, Babalao slamming the front door on his way out. Joe takes a breath of air. Then, while still on one knee, he sheathes his sword, placing it back in its scabbard. He gets up to a standing position as his friend Herbie lands softly on his right shoulder.

"Let me help you, Amanda," Joe says. He grabs a cloth and starts wiping down the table full of coffee and coffee cup pieces.

"Joe! My friend Joe," Herbie says proudly.

Amelia says, "Wow, some people are way out on Halloween night! Thank you, sweetie, but I'll finish cleaning up."

Joe and Amelia suddenly hear noise outside, the sound of people frantically screaming in the street. "Stay inside, Amelia, please!" Joe instructs. He quickly steps outside the organic coffee shop, with Herbie on his left shoulder. Everyone outside, including children who are dressed in Halloween costumes, is screaming in horror, "Aaaah!" as they witness three male zombies eating Hamburger, the merchant's security guard.

Hamburger says faintly, "Must save the children." He dies pinned against a car parked on Rodeo Drive. The hungry zombies, making snorting noises like pigs, turn their attention toward Joe. They drop the body of the brave security guard who gave his life for the children who were in harm's way. The zombies walk awkwardly in Joe's direction, hungry for more human flesh.

Herbie's eyes open up wide. "Look out, Joe!" Herbie says. Joe lifts his front arm high, which elevates his body. He cocks his right leg into his chest, pushing off with his left foot to move forward, launching a powerful side kick into the closest zombie's torso. *Thud!* With that zombie propelled backward into the other zombie, both zombies go down like dominoes to the ground.

Another zombie is trying to grab Herbie, who is in the air above Joe. "Err!" the zombie growls.

"Bad zombie. Awk!" Herbie says. He distracts the zombie for Joe. Suddenly, the zombie's head gets lopped off by Joe's sword. Two other zombies go walking away, heading back toward Babalao, who is waiting for them in the dark alley. Peace has been restored, it seems, on Rodeo Drive.

Everyone hears police sirens in the distance coming toward the area. Joe flicks his sword to the ground as the zombie's blood falls off, completing a chiburi. Then he re-sheathes his sword, placing it back into his scabbard. Joe says, "Let's walk into the alley, Herbie."

"Kidding, Joe." Herbie gulps. "Stay close to the wall, Joe," Herbie advises. Joe enters the alley and glides close to the dark wall. A hungry zombie attempts to bite Joe's arms and hands, but Joe elbows the zombie's forehead. *Plop!* It explodes, splashing blood and white pus onto Joe's face and onto Herbie's wings.

"Yuk," Herbie says.

Another zombie, from the shadows, comes at Joe, growling with hunger for human flesh: *"Rrr!"* Joe lifts his leg quickly and fluidly to do a Wing Chun front kick, thrusting the zombie backward a few feet into some trash cans. The zombie attempts to regain his balance. Joe's springy legs jump from a standing position, vaulting him high off the ground, and he delivers a side kick to the zombie's face. *Pow!* Joe lands on the ground softly like a cat, and then spins on the ball of one foot, his other leg tucked close to his body and exploding into full extension, generating power to kick into the zombie's abdomen. *Poof!*

The zombie spits smelly bluish foam from his mouth and stumbles backward. Then Joe, from a few feet away, uses extreme concentration to do a side-shuffle step in the zombie's direction. Joe releases his ki and let's loose a yell: "Kia!" Joe's side-shuffle step produces a powerful side kick, launching the zombie twenty feet backward. The zombie falls hard, landing against a big Dumpster. *Thud!*

The undead zombie, on the ground and foaming at the mouth, with evil intent, attempts to get up again, but Herbie swoops down. *Swat!* He hits the zombie's nose hard with his parrot feet. The zombie, unable to feel pain, grabs some of Herbie's feathers. "Wa-irk!" Herbie screams. Joe dropkicks the zombie's face—*smack!*—as if trying to make a sixty-yard field goal. Blood mixed with zombie pus shoots up into the air as the zombie's head disconnects from its body and flies far to the other end of the alley, landing inside a Dumpster. "Field goal!" Herbie shouts.

Joe, adrenaline pumping, feels that something is still there in the dark. *It's Babalao,* Joe thinks. He pulls out his archangel holy sword and readies for the coup de grâce. As Joe is focused on finding Babalao, Baka, the evil beast dog with the keen stealth hunting skills of a coyote, creeps close to Joe, baring its huge teeth. Herbie suddenly attacks Baka's eyes fiercely with his talons. "Joe!" Herbie shouts. Baka, blinded from the attack, somehow gets Herbie inside his mouth. Herbie struggles not to be eaten.

"*No!*" Joe shouts. He brings his sword down for a *kesagiri* (diagonal cut), lopping Baka's head clean off.

"Wow … awk! Close one, Joe," Herbie gratefully says as he squirms out of Baka's mouth. Joe breathes a partial sigh of relief, as Joe's sixth sense still tells him that danger—something evil—is near.

Their sirens blasting, some Beverly Hills police officers arrive, flashing their high beams into the alley, professionally taking charge of the scene. "We got this, Joe!" the police sergeant commands.

Papa Legba! A sudden eerie noise comes from a trash dumpster. Wind and trash fly in the air, smacking the officers in the face. They pull out their handguns. The sergeant has his shotgun cocked and ready to shoot. The high beams from their vehicles go out. Some scramble to turn on their flashlights. *Papa Legba* sounds come from the abyss. Suddenly Babalao leaps out of the trash Dumpster. He has transformed into a zombie with vampire or pit bull teeth. He swings his cane, attempting to bite anything human. *Bam! Bam! Bam!* Officers unload their weapons into Babalao. Then, *kaboom!* The police sergeant blasts his twelve-gauge shotgun, blowing off some of Babalao's head. Greenish-red zombie pus splatters all over the officers' faces and uniforms. "Doggone it! Another human on Halloween night freebasing on over-the-counter bath salts," the police sergeant says. "Quickly, Joe." Joe, using economy of motion, places his holy sword in its sheath on the left side of his waistband.

"Salts? You blind. Awk!" Herbie says. Then Joe gives his statement about what transpired, as do many other witnesses.

The police sergeant says, "Joe, you're a hero. So is the dead security guard. Hey, Joe, your sword sure looks like the real McCoy."

Another police officer says, obviously defending Joe, "Ease

up, Sergeant! You have to be dressed up like Robin Hood or a knight to walk the streets on Halloween night, right?" The police sergeant smiles and nods his head. He and the other officers, both men and women, clean the zombie blood and pus from their faces. Yet they suspiciously wonder why Joe appears to have a real sword. Joe, knowing what they're thinking, just smiles. He does not answer any questions. With Herbie on his left shoulder, he walks away with *zanshin* (warrior spirit).

The Beverly Hills CSI crew arrives to do evidence recovery and then conduct a quick cleanup so that Halloween night can keep rolling. The thirsty police sergeant quickly disappears into the organic coffee shop to finish cleaning up in the restroom. Then he grabs a cup of joe. He sees the clean police lieutenant sitting down drinking coffee. "Been there, done that!" the lieutenant says, laughing at the sergeant.

Down the road a mite on this horrific Halloween night is Jesse, whom we know is a country boy. He happens to be a new police officer in Beverly Hills, California. There isn't much work back home for Jesse, because wildlife, including fish, have been depleted on account of the world's population growth. Jesse decided to go to the big city to get work, and send money back home every month to help with his large family's expenses. As Jesse drives his patrol car, he remembers his grandpa Luke, who just recently passed away, warning him about the evil in the big city and telling him to be very careful. Jesse figures he'll do twenty years as a cop and then retire back to the hills, where all his kinfolk are.

Jesse is suddenly called via police radio dispatch, with instructions to identify a subject fitting the description of a big man wearing a funny Halloween mask and running with a real knife that is dripping with blood. *Hmm,* Jesse thinks. Driving by some new dance disco joint called Club Saman, Jesse sees Joe, with his parrot Herbie on his shoulder, headed in that direction. "Wow! That place is sure rocking! But I have an uneasy feeling. I guess that's the country boy in me," Jesse says as he continues to drive past the flashing lights of Club Saman. Driving around the corner into a residential neighborhood, he sees a man wearing a funny-looking Halloween mask that shows his huge ugly yellowish fungus-like teeth, which are protruding outside the mask. The man, seeing Officer Jesse approaching the scene, laughs wildly at first, and then growls like a jackal: "Arrr!" He then runs into the rumored Beverly Hills Haunted Mansion on Halloween night. Jesse contemplates whether he should call for backup per protocol. He knows backup will be approximately ten to thirty minutes away, given the high crime on Halloween night. Beverly Hills was recently hit with budget cuts, so now the force has fewer police officers. "It seems to have the Devil's stamp of approval," the local church reverend had said at the town meeting. *But that's politics,* according to Jesse, whose keen awareness and country hunting ears pick up the scream of a woman inside the haunted mansion. Jesse says, "What the hell?! I'd better go inside and help the woman!" He attempts to use his police radio to request backup, but apparently the radio's battery is dead. "What? You've got to be kidding. And it's Halloween night too. I could have sworn this radio's battery was fully charged," Jesse says.

The highly trained police officer cautiously approaches the house. As he opens the squeaking front door—*eek*—he draws his police-issue 9 mm handgun with a twenty-round magazine. With his other hand, he places his flashlight with his gun—combining the two by connecting his two wrists like a cross. "I wish I had a cross or a Bible with me," Jesse says to himself.

Looking around, the officer sees no one. Looking up, he observes light coming from beneath the door of the upstairs bedroom.

"*Meow!*" a smelly black cat cries from two feet away, looking at Jesse.

Breathing hard, Jesse says to himself, "Settle down. Settle down." The large black tomcat, howling and then coughing, shows no fear of the officer. Suddenly, a huge man appears with big saucer eyes wearing a funny-looking mask with protruding stained ugly teeth, and sewer-smelling foul breath that immediately gives Officer Jesse an instant headache. He begins dangerously walking toward the officer, saying, "I'm Beelzebub, and you're mine!"

As the man continues to walk in Jesse's direction, Jesse shouts orders: "No! Stop! Get down on the ground! On your belly!"

The big man who calls himself Beelzebub shows his ugly protruding teeth, as if to bite Officer Jesse through his evil-looking Mesoamerican mask. He continues walking in Jesse's direction without fear, wielding a large sharp-looking knife. With dark smelly bloodstains, his huge evil feet make sounds on the floor like bricks—*Clump! Clump! Clump!* Smelling toxic breath coming from the mouth hole of the Mesoamerican mask, Jesse, with his heart pounding, starts shooting bullets point-blank at the horrible man, but Beelzebub keeps coming toward him, the bullets striking him but doing no harm. Jesse says, "God help me!"

The huge evil man somehow drops his knife. He grunts furiously, a sound from hell, as he clenches his fists. Then he swings his huge right fist at Jesse, releasing his powerful energy from the abyss, striking Officer Jesse extremely hard on the right side of his face. *Crack!* Jesse feels and hears his face bones break and pop, which causes him instant excruciating pain. He falls to the ground. Jesse, delirious and with blurred vision, sees the evil man pick up his huge knife and start walking over to him. Jesse knows the man is going to kill him, so he prays for God not to let him feel the cold steel death strike.

Joe suddenly enters the room. *Clank!* Joe's sword knocks the big knife out of Beelzebub's hands. Beelzebub quickly jumps forward, lunging into Joe's legs, wrapping his arms around them and taking Joe to the ground, knocking Joe's sword a few feet away. As Beelzebub is atop Joe, Herbie flies through the air and says, "Jesse hurt, Joe. Awk!" Beelzebub swings his clenched fists downward, striking Joe's face and grazing other parts of his body.

Joe moves, determined not to stay still. He remembers his sensei Musashi saying, "Joe, you must move when on the ground with your opponent. If you lie still like a dead dog, you will die like a dog!"

Joe, underneath Beelzebub, curls his foot to trap one of Beelzebub's feet and legs, grabs the arm on the same side of his body as the trapped leg, and shouts, "Oompah!" Joe raises his waist, with leverage forcing Beelzebub to fall forward and to the side. Joe gets on top of Beelzebub, mounting him so that now he is the attacker. Joe unleashes powerful bare-knuckle strikes onto Beelzebub's face. *Pop! Kapow! Crack!* He knocks Beelzebub's mask off, revealing a demonic presence. Beelzebub rolls over onto his belly to avoid Joe's punishing knuckle blows. Joe, still on top, quickly wraps his arms around Beelzebub's neck for a rear choke. He thinks he is squeezing the life out of the evil man, but this person cannot be choked out, which seems abnormal to Joe.

Joe uses his knees to guide Beelzebub close to where Joe can reach for his sword. Beelzebub reaches for Joe's sword, but Herbie lands on Beelzebub's arm in midreach and furiously pecks away at it.

"Arrh!" Beelzebub growls in pain. Joe uses his left hand to keep Beelzebub down. He grabs his sword with his right hand, quickly raises it over Beelzebub's head, and then, using only his right hand, drops his sword downward for a *shitamuki-no* strike, lopping off Beelzebub's head. It rolls like a ball over to Jesse's left thigh, into which it bites deep with demonic presence.

"Aar!" Jesse screams in pain. A few minutes later, Officer Jesse awakes on a gurney, as he's being placed into an ambulance. Good thing Joe used his royal cell phone to contact the emergency medical team.

Joe calmly says, "You're in good hands, Jesse." Finally, the police backup force arrived.

Herbie says, "Joe ... let's go! Awk! Help Rose."

"Sure, little buddy." Joe walks briskly back to town, with Herbie perched on his left shoulder.

As Beverly Hills' finest observe the medical emergency team attending to Officer Jesse, one of the EMTs says, "It's just Halloween night, with typical drama again."

The police sergeant, Bully, says, "I wish you would have waited for backup, Jesse!"

One of the other officers says, "Hey, ease up, Sergeant. You know that the policy is that officers must do first-responder action! It's a no-brainer. An officer will get fired if they wait for backup these days, remember?"

As Officer Jesse looks at his brother officers for comfort, tears come down his face. He is saddened because he knows that he will not be able to make the date with Amelia. He also weeps over the violent horror he was victim to. The young officer has a look of traumatized distress on his face as the ambulance speeds him off to the nearest hospital. The ambulance driver's partner, who is sitting in the back with Officer Jesse, studies the patient's face and says, "You look like you've just lost a date with a beautiful angel. But all is not lost ... I found something on the ground outside." Then the emergency medical technician reaches for a hideous mask on the floor and puts it on his face. Suddenly, his face metamorphoses. Ugly teeth protrude from the mouth of the mask. With glowing red eyes, the EMT, who is sitting next to Officer Jesse, begins to laugh devilishly with evil intent. "Ha-ha, hu-hu, he-he."

Officer Jesse screams, "Nooo!" on this Halloween night, as they roar down the road en route to the nearest hospital.

CHAPTER 5

Later that Halloween night at Club Saman, now that she has finished with her babysitting duties, Rose arrives for her appointment to meet with the owner and manager of Club Saman to discuss a possible music performance. She waits in line at the entrance, while the hypnotically alluring bright red lights flash, spelling out "Saman. Saman." Rose observes that posted on both sides of Club Saman's large entrance are two huge men wearing black robes with hoods over their heads, thus making it impossible to see their faces. Rose hears mysterious animal sounds coming from them. Also, customers walking by them hear what seems to be noise from nasal mucus, kind of like the sounds a pig would make. As Rose moves forward in line, she finds herself right below the enchanting flashing red Saman entrance sign. Curiously, as some people walk by the two huge bouncers, one of them blurts out, "Hey, big guy, what do the fine-print words say below the Saman sign?"

Immediately, the larger bouncer turns his big body to face the incoming customer. "*Shut up, human!*" The other bouncer grunts, motioning with his powerful arms for the patrons to keep moving and enter the club.

Rose, looking up, spots another sign that reads, "Enter at your own risk. All human beings have freewill choice. Club

Saman is not liable, in any way, shape, or form, for anything, including any physical or mental injuries that might result in death while you're inside Club Saman."

Rose thinks, *So many businesses are afraid of lawsuits.* As she pays her cover to enter, she observes other people placing their right hands on top of a computer that suddenly lights up with a red glow—the human chip implant. *Bam!* Sounds the computer. A mysterious controlled look comes across the faces of these people. Then they walk into Club Saman without paying the cover. (Revelation 13:17: "To be branded with a mark of the beast on the right hand.") Upon entering the club, Rose hears alluring music playing and observes people dancing hypnotically. Walking around the club, she sees people smoking authorized marijuana cigarettes, smoking hashish through a soda can, or drinking two bottles of liquor at the same time, both bottles inside their mouths!

What? I wish Joe were here. Where is the manager or the owner? I will certainly, without reservation, depart these premises if I do not make contact with him soon. My brave brother says, "Do not be afraid of walking into the lions' den if it's the Father's calling," Rose thinks. She is approached by a hostess of Club Saman, who asks her to sit down in one of the guest seats near the entrance. Rose sits. The hostess says, "I will convey your message. I will convey your message." The hostess then walks away in a robotic demeanor.

Suddenly, a young woman shouts, "Hey! Where's my fiancé, Big Jimbo? He never came back from the restroom."

One of Jimbo's friends says, "Yeah, man. He's one tough United States Marine Corps brother. But let's go see what happened to Big Jimbo!" Several young men and women, friends of Jimbo, get up from their seats and go searching for their friend. As Jimbo's friends arrive at the men's and women's restrooms, they see a line of people, so they get in line.

As people move forward in line, they see huge men wearing dark robes with hoods that cover their faces, grim reaper style. These horrific, mysterious-looking men instruct, "Have the woman nurse at the table insert our special Club Saman human RFID chip in your right hand, please!" (Revelation 13:17: "To be branded with a mark of the beast on the right hand.") Some of the people agree, and are allowed to enter the restrooms. However, the ones who refuse the chip implant, which is intended to become part of their body, are instructed to walk down a dimly lit corridor to the other restrooms. When this happens, the huge hooded men grumble.

One of Jimbo's friends says, "Screw that, G! Bang your head on the wall! There's nobody putting a chip in my hand! We're just in here looking for our friend Big Jimbo! He came here to visit us from the farm. Since he just received his honorable discharge from the United States Marine Corps, you all are lucky we didn't bring our pieces with us."

Then, one of Jimbo's country hillbilly friends says, "Golly and shazam! What we gonna do?"

Jimbo's Chicano friend says, *"No sé. Los vamos, mis amigos!"* (I don't know. Let's get out of here, my friends!)

A Japanese friend of Jimbo says, *"Kurutteru. Koko kara demashou."* (This is crazy. Let's get out of here.)

A Chinese friend of Jimbo says, *"Zhe tai fengkuangle. Rang women gankuai likai zheli."* (This is crazy. Let's get out of here.)

Then, a Filipino friend of Jimbo says, *"Ito ay mabaliw. Nagbibigay-daan sa makakuha ng out sa ditto."* (This is crazy. Let's get out of here.)

Then, Jimbo's big German friend says, *"Das is verruckt. Lass uns von hier verschwinden."* (This is crazy. Let's get out of here.)

A handsome young man who is a military officer and the natural leader of Jimbo's friends suggests, "This isn't rocket science. Everyone, listen up. We must exit this establishment as a team now!"

"Yeah, man, let's roll out of here!" someone from the group says.

Jimbo's fiancée sobs, "But I love my Big Jimbo. Please help me find him!" All of Big Jimbo's friends then decide not to leave. They are all team players, so they precede to the other bathrooms, walking down the yellow corridor—the walls, floor, and ceiling all yellow, with blinding bright purple lights flashing on the floor—as instructed by the female nurse with the face of a pig and mysterious glowing eyes.

At the end of the corridor, Jimbo's friends enter just past a sliding soundproof door. The door immediately locks behind them. They frightfully hear screams of pain ahead. Worried, one of Big Jimbo's friends double checks the sliding door behind them, "Hey, they locked us in here. My cell phone doesn't work inside here either."

Jimbo's friends, although in a panic, continue to walk forward. They are horrified to witness huge men with pig facial features snorting pig sounds while grabbing people and pulling them into a back room. *Bam!* These people are having their limbs broken with baseball bats, which are being used to bludgeon their heads, faces, and other body parts. All of Big Jimbo's friends attempt to escape, but their efforts are in vain. They become victims once they are overpowered by huge pig-faced grim reaper men who have the strength of a devil on this Halloween night.

Jimbo's fiancée finally sees his body on a heap of bodies that have been bludgeoned to death. She screams.

"Your body is God's temple, where the spirit of God dwells. Anyone who destroys their body destroys God's temple, therefore they themselves will be destroyed" (Corinthians 3:16).

Away from the restroom area, Rose is seated near the dance

floor. She patiently awaits the arrival of the manager of Club Saman. Mysteriously, the dance music changes. The people feel a powerful presence. Then suddenly, on the balcony, a very handsome man wearing an expensive custom-made suit appears, overlooking everyone below, including Rose. Rose gazes up in awe of the magnetism this man projects. She suddenly feels an attraction. The man spots her looking at him and breaks into a huge smile. He waves at her with his right hand, on which he is wearing a Water Mason ring. He then slowly walks downstairs, avoiding and ignoring the other people, focused only on Rose. As he walks smoothly, she moves her eyes to the handsome magnate's shoes, to see if they match his debonair suit. His shoes are one of a kind, impeccable handmade crocodile dress shoes from John Lobb's of England.

"Hello, madam! My name is Edward DiCaprio. I'm the owner of this establishment. May I help you?" Edward says.

Rose shakes his hand, then says, "You have a ring similar to my late grandfather's. Have I seen you somewhere before, Mr. DiCaprio?"

"I have seen you before, Rose. Edward. Please just call me Edward!"

Rose asks, "Where have you seen me, Edward?"

"Well, Rose, please allow me an opportunity to share something of a dichotomy. When I first saw you, Miss Rose, you were playing a grand piano while singing like a songbird at a benefit concert here in Beverly Hills. I was much younger then. The memory of you was burned into my subconscious, as was the treasured memory of my late parents, whom I was accompanied by that evening," Edward cordially says.

As Rose and Edward continue their conversation, with obvious chemistry between them Edward senses Rose is uncomfortable in the club. "This place isn't for you, Rose. Would you like to step outside, so we can plan your benefit concert, which will certainly not be here at Club Saman? I assure you, Miss Rose," Edward says.

"Yes, Edward, you've read my mind. Please, yes, Edward, you may escort me outside for a brief moment."

At that moment, Joe enters Club Saman, passing through the front entrance unchecked by the bouncers, and unnoticed by the Saman hand-chip reader. Finding his sister, he asks, "Rose, where are you going? And with whom?"

"Joe. This is Edward. Edward, this is my brother, Joe."

As both men shake hands, Edward says, "Joe, your handshake feels unusual. Have we met before?"

"Maybe. … Where are you going with my sister?"

"Outside, Joe. This place is not really, in my opinion, appropriate for a lady such as your sister, Rose," Edward says.

Rose says, "Please do not worry, Joe. My mission in life is to bring celestial music to calm people's souls."

Herbie jumps on Edward's shoulder and sniffs him. "He's okay, Joe. Awk!" Herbie says.

"Well, I trust you will bring my sister, Rose, home—not too late …"

"Before midnight, Joe! I promise to take good care of your sister."

"Good," Joe says.

"And, Joe, these restrooms are not for you. They need refurbishing. Please go across the street if you need the restroom," Edward recommends.

"The restrooms? Hmm … yes, the restrooms, Edward."

"Good-bye, Joe," Rose says, kissing her brother on his cheek. Then Edward motions his big bodyguards who are wearing wrestling masks to move people out of their way, so he and Rose can easily head outside to his limousine parked in front. Edward and Rose both walk outside.

Meanwhile, inside Club Saman, Herbie, flapping his parrot wings, says, "Restroom, Joe. Irk!"

"You recommend we go to the restroom, Herbie?" Joe questions. He agrees. Herbie jumps on Joe's left shoulder as he proceeds in the direction of the restrooms. Joe's sixth sense tells him there is danger ahead, so he grips his sword handle as he walks toward the restrooms. He remembers his sensei Musashi saying, "Joe, never be off guard. Be ready for whatever may come!"

Meanwhile, Rose and Edward are just outside Club Saman. Edward asks, "Would you like to accompany me inside my limo and talk, Rose? It's more private than out here, where there's people all around. We don't have to go anywhere if you don't desire. Just sitting inside the limo, we could hear each other better than inside the club." Edward pulls a Cuban cigar from his pocket, lighting it with his handmade solid-gold lighter from Africa. Good thing Cuba has reconciled with the United States, an event that is spearheading a possible one world order.

With impatience, Rose looks at Edward. Smiling like the beautiful angel that she is, she attempts to look deep into Edward's mind. Edward smiles as he puffs vigorously on his Cuban cigar, which envelops Edward and Rose in a private aura of smoke.

Sensing a staring game, Edward says impressively, "Rose, would you prefer that I call you a cab? And please, let it be at my expense, no matter where you desire to go."

"No. I prefer to sit in your limo and talk to you, Edward," Rose says. They continue to walk toward the limo.

The head bodyguard walks up to them, holds out his right palm, and says, "Excuse me, Mr. DiCaprio, sir, but your old chauffeur is a little sick, and lazy too. Would you like me to take over the duty of driving your limousine, sir?"

"No! He's fine!" Edward, frustrated about the derogatory comment, accidentally puts his cigar out on his bodyguard's open palm.

"*Ouch!*" the bodyguard screams.

"Listen up! Don't ever make comments about my chauffeur again! Understood?" Edward commands. The head bodyguard, frightened, bows, while holding his burned palm hand, and takes a few steps backward. Edward opens the limousine door like a gentleman for Rose.

"Thank you, Edward."

"You're most welcome, Rose," Edward says.

Once they are both inside the limousine, the chauffeur, who is an old man in a finely dressed suit, says, "Hello, Bubo! May I drive you and your lovely lady friend to some quiet but elegant restaurant?"

"No, Grandfather. Not just yet. Just leave this area please, and sort of drive around. Thank you, Grandfather!" Edward says. The limo departs the area.

Meanwhile, back inside Club Saman, Joe approaches the restrooms. The lady at the table just outside the restroom grunts like a pig, and motions for Joe to have a RFID computer chip placed in his right hand. Joe also motions with his index finger, indicating no. He continues walking, and reaches a yellow corridor with blinding purple flashing lights on the floor. Two huge bodyguards follow Joe. Herbie says, "Joe! Behind us. Awk!"

"I know, my fine feathered friend … stay loose," Joe says. Suddenly, upon reaching the end of the yellow corridor and reaching the unassigned restrooms, Joe beholds a horrible sight, four huge men with dark hoods over their faces striking and grabbing young men and women. As one of these huge men walks up to Joe and then reaches for him, Joe unsheathes his sword. With both hands on the handle, he swings for a rising cut—*migigyaku kesa*—swings his sword from left to right, rising slightly as if swinging for a home run! With this, he cuts the big man in half. *Flop!* The upper torso falls to the ground, with blood spilling everywhere. The two men attempt to grab Joe from behind, but he spins around 180 degrees with his sword to cut *suihei-no*—horizontally, for a neck cut, called a *nekku*, lopping off both assailants' heads. Joe then turns his sword to the ground for a chiburi, flicking the blood off the blade.

Joe shouts, "Run!" The men and women attempt to run, but, afraid, they stop in shock, as a very huge man the size of an elephant, his facial features resembling a pig combined with a wild boar, comes from the back room. Following him are two other two big men, wearing dark hoods over their heads to cover their faces. The two big men toss off their hoods and reveal pig facial features. The biggest man, the size of an elephant, rushes Joe. Calmly, Joe breathes in air, and then unleashes his sword quickly for a mixture of horizontal (*suihei*) and vertical (*suichoku*) cuts, making seven separate cuts in all. The big man falls in seven huge pieces to the floor, completing a *roku-dan giri*.

Herbie shouts a commanding, "Joe!"

The two other big men scream, "Oink! Oink!"

Joe shouts to everyone, "Run! Get out!" The men and women immediately run toward the exit door. Then, the two other two big men, not nearly the size of an elephant like their fallen comrade, raise their billy clubs and attack Joe with the intent to kill. Joe does two quick vertical strikes, one up and one down, and cuts off both assailants' hands. *Plop!* Blood flies through the air like paint at a paint shop as the billy clubs with the severed hands fall to the floor. The men fearfully flee away from Joe, screaming in pain, "Oink! Oink!"

"Joe! Awk!" Herbie, concerned, says. Joe has greenish-brownish-red blood all over him from the assailants who looked like pigs.

"What were those, Herbie?" Joe asks.

Herbie flaps his wings and shakes his head in bewilderment. He suggests, "Clean up, Joe."

Joe nods his head in agreement. They saunter over to the restroom sink.

Meanwhile, Rose and Edward are enjoying the chemistry between them as they talk together in the immaculate limo. The chauffeur smiles and then closes the dividing window so that his grandson may have some privacy with the young lady.

"I enjoyed your inspiring concert years ago at the Benson Foundation fund-raiser. My parents took me there when they were alive. Now all I have is my grandfather, who is my personal chauffeur. Rose, would you like to drink some bottled water from my company?" Edward says.

"Yes, thank you," Rose says. She opens the water bottle, drinks, and then says, "Mm ... good. Yes, Edward, I remember you now! You kept waving hi to me from the audience, but you kept your distance. And now you have me sitting next to you, Edward."

"Rose, I've been busy with the family business, Saman Industries, since my parents' unfortunate passing," Edward says with a sigh of grief.

"Edward, we seem to have something in common. We've both lost our parents. However, you seem to have come a long way, Edward." Changing the subject, Rose says, "The water in the bottle feels very nourishing ... why?"

"The bottle is made out of glass for purposes of longevity. The water was bottled from Mount Everest, a well several miles deep into the earth with water full of minerals from ancient times. It as water was meant to be drunk. A thousand dollars a bottle it costs!

"I'm glad you remember me, Rose. I always thought you were a down-to-earth girl, and I somehow knew that being a world entertainer wouldn't change you, Rose. However, I personally have a strange dualism within myself, something of a dichotomy," Edward responds.

Rose pauses. "Why does your grandfather, who is also very sweet, call you Bubo?" Rose inquires.

"Only for you, Rose, will I answer that question. My full name is Edward Bubo Dicaprio. I know you are wondering why my grandfather, who is eighty years old, is my chauffeur. My grandfather is my only living relative since my parents died tragically in a car crash when their brakes mysteriously went out. I can trust my grandfather. And he is old, but he does a great job, and makes interesting conversation on the way to all my board meetings."

Rose says, "Very expensive, Edward, your bottled water; however, it is really quite exquisite. It has the Saman name on it."

"I can explain, Rose. As far as bottled water, well, my company is a corporation that seems to feel that owning the world's water supply will mean *power*! My father, when he was alive, practiced dungeon politics, or so he called it, with the Water Masons when I was child. He never had much time for me, and my mother would never interfere, as she was a Stepford wife. My grandfather, aware of this, started taking me on fishing trips. One day at Lake Los Carneros in Santa Barbara, California, a big horned owl landed on a tree branch near to us and kept looking at me. My grandfather told me that the horned owl picked me to be his familiar, saying that from that point on I would do great in school! He also said that I would accomplish great things, things that no other person had done before! Well, I don't know if my grandfather told me that as a placebo, but when I went back to school, I excelled in my studies, earning straight A's from then on. Sometimes, mysteriously, a horned owl would land nearby me, so my late father requested that his powerful Water Mason brothers have a small horned owl placed on the front of the one-dollar bill," Edward Bubo Dicaprio says. Edward, using a magnifying glass, shows Rose the front of the US dollar bill where George Washington's face is. "You see, Rose, right here at the top right is the number 1, and above it a little, slightly to the left, you see a horned owl. And please, I would like to fulfill the prophecies, so I prefer that you call me Bubo!" Edward says.

"Yes, Bubo. I see a little horned owl a little to the left on above top-right number 1. Amazing. I never knew," Rose says. She continues, "This is all interesting, Bubo, but what about the Water Masons?"

Bubo looks at an incoming text on his cell phone watch. It contains information regarding Rose's late grandfather General Arnold Benson, and his high-ranking Water Mason affiliation. With the attraction building between the two of them, Bubo looks into Rose's enchanting eyes. "In special circumstances, I am allowed to inform you that the Water Masons are a secret organized society. I know your grandfather was a member of this organization; therefore, I feel allowed to court you, if you would graciously allow me, Rose," Bubo says, going down on one knee on the floor of the limo and looking into Rose's eyes.

"Yes, Bubo!" she says, laughing. "As for now, will you please give me a ride home? I do not wish to have any problems be-tween you and my brother, Joe," Rose warmly says.

"Your brother, Joe, looks very athletic. I do not want any problems with him either. Thank you, Rose, for allowing me to have more time with you on this Halloween night. Please, Rose, type in your address on this direction finder that is connected to my grandfather's system. My company is working very hard on computer drone RFID chips, and DNA drone chips for humans." Pressing the bottom to have the divider window slide down, Bubo says, "Hey, Grandpa, please take your time. Don't rush." Bubo laughing. His grandpa laughs, raising his right hand, which is implanted with a human chip, to motion his satisfaction.

Rose types her home address on a small electric pad that is connected to the chauffeur's earpiece. She then gets a call on her cell phone. It's Joe. "Yes, Brother. I'm all right, Joe. Mr. Edward Bubo DiCaprio is giving me a ride home from the Club Saman. We have been just driving around and around while talking, getting acquainted with one another. I'm fine, Joe," Rose reassures.

"Oh yeah? Well, please tell him thank you, and mention that I will talk to him soon, one-on-one! And Rose, please stay away from Club Saman! I worry about you," Joe says.

Herbie shouts "Stay away Saman! Rose! Awk."

"Okay, Joe and Herbie. I love you both. Good-bye," Rose says.

Joe also says his good-byes, and places his royal cell phone in his pocket. He turns back to washing his face and hands in the restroom sink. So does Herbie, taking a swan dive into the full sink of water Joe has prepared for him. He washes his parrot head, feet, and feathers. There is peace in Club Saman, for now at least ...

Meanwhile, the limousine arrives at Benson Manor. The chauffeur grandfather opens the door for Rose and Bubo. "Here you are, milady, Miss Rose, and you too, Grandson," Bubo's grandfather says. Always the gentleman, Bubo escorts Rose to the manor door. Joe senses their arrival. At the steps leading up to the front door, Rose and Bubo stop. It seems both of them are reluctant to open the front door, which will end their Halloween night together. However, the front door opens. "Hello!" Joe says.

"Joe, this is Edward again. And Edward, this is my brother

Joe again," Rose says. Edward and Joe shake hands. Edward tests Joe by squeezing hard; however, Joe releases the pressure of Edward's hand by squeezing hard, which causes one of Edward's knuckles to crack. *Pop!* After all, Joe's right hand is his sword hand, his strongest. Immediately Rose says, "There now, gentlemen." Joe smiles. He can't help but notice Edward has a Water Mason ring on his finger, just like the one his grandfather wore.

"It's a pleasure to meet you again, Joe. And truthfully, speaking from my heart, I take comfort in making sure Rose arrived home safely on this Halloween night," Edward says.

"Yes, I thank you, sir. Good-bye!" Joe says.

"Well, I'll be rushing off now that you're safely home, Rose. Is there a possibility that I may be honored to have your gracious presence in the near future, Rose?" Edward courteously requests in Joe's presence, keeping Joe in his peripheral vision. It seems to Rose, though, that she's admired by this confident magnate called Edward Bubo Dicaprio.

"Why, yes, Edward! Please call me soon," Rose says. She gives Bubo her cell phone number.

"Good-bye, sir!" Herbie says, also with confidence. Everyone laughs.

The magnate gets into his limousine. It speeds away on this Halloween night.

As Rose goes to sleep, Joe slips out of the house with Herbie to do some more rounds around town, since Halloween night isn't officially over yet.

Back at Club Saman, a waitress comes up to a sharp-dressed war veteran. "Hey, sir, I noticed that you have positioned yourself so that you can see the front door, the restrooms, and the balcony here at Club Saman, and that you haven't drunk or smoked anything the whole time you've been here. Maybe you should go into the men's restroom down that corridor, where they have many things like chocolate candy, narcotics, and female companionship." the waitress says.

"Well, it's like this, missy. From this spot I can spot all the chicks and hoodlums who come and go, and I don't drink in a place I go into for the first time, and I don't smoke weed, because then I can't fight. I am a hunter, a warrior, so I don't pay whores! I'm a conqueror using my charm. I'm a man of the world, an ex-military war veteran, sister!"

"Oh, one of those. Okay, sir," the waitress says. Then she walks away, talking into her wireless microphone and listening through the earpiece.

The war veteran is sitting in a dimly lit corner. He wonders… *Why is it very few women and men come out of the restroom? I don't care about the men really, but the pretty chicks can't stay back there forever. There must be a hell of a party going on inside those restrooms.* "Oh yeah, I remember now! It's Halloween night!" the war veteran says. "Hey, here comes a chick now from the restroom. Hey, baby, how about that slow, slow dance? I don't bite!" the war veteran inquires, testosterone kicking strong in his blood.

She says, "Name's Ruth."

"Name's Rooster—and a male rooster is called a cock," Rooster says.

"Oh yeah? Are you cock-strong war veteran?" The athletic young woman puckers her mouth and moves in close to the veteran, who is seated in an area several feet away from the long tunnel that leads to the restroom entrance.

"Yeah, Ruth, baby. Who's your daddy?" the fierce-looking war veteran proclaims in a rough voice. Ruth kisses Rooster on his cheek. He hugs her voluptuous body. All of a sudden, he feels extreme pain and heat on his neck. Tilting his head away to see what she's doing, he smells a foul odor coming from her mouth.

Then he sees her large pointed rotten vampire teeth with his blood on them.

"Get away, bitch!" the war veteran shouts, attempting to push her off him.

However, on this Halloween night, she is very powerful. She continues to hold him in the corner while sucking out his blood. It sounds like a straw sucking up a beverage. "Mm! This is delicious!" the vampire woman says, as the veteran's eyes flicker from lack of blood.

Suddenly, Joe spots what is happening, as he has just entered the area. Herbie flies up high into the air, and Joe does a rear martial art jujutsu choke hold on the vampire lady, pulling her off the war veteran on this Halloween night.

Ruth has many lotions and creams on her cold body. She slips out of Joe's clutches and then jumps high to swat Herbie. *Slap!* Bird feathers explode all around as Herbie says, "Awk!" Joe senses she's up in the dark ceiling, but he cannot see her. Then Ruth lands softly behind Joe, creeping up on him to launch a surprise attack.

Joe says, "My sixth sense feels danger, but where's Herbie?" Unbeknownst to Joe, Herbie is on a ledge above, shaking off his injuries. Ruth grabs Joe from behind, attempting to bite his neck. But Joe can control his attacker's ki, which is the inner spirit, driving force, or center of energy. Ruth has committed herself to a course of action, and has also committed her ki, which is directed toward that end. Joe reaches behind his body with his right hand, which he places beneath Ruth's armpit. He bends forward to judo-flip Ruth's body and redirect it into an executive table filled with champagne and caviar.

Splash! Joe cracks a smile as the men and women from that table, doctors, lawyers, businessmen, politicians, and an NBA star, swing their fists at Ruth, striking her. Ruth squirms off the table, disappearing into an unlighted area. The important people then have a huge bowl of fondue with bread brought to the table. The waitress takes off the lid. The basketball star tosses a piece of bread that hits the rim of the bowl, then falls in. The politician says, "You need a big swoosh, big guy." They all laugh.

The waitress is about to depart the table. The basketball star says, "You could put a basketball in that big bowl. Thank you, waitress."

The waitress says, "You're welcome. You're welcome." She walks away, making unhuman snorting sounds like those of a pig.

Herbie now lands softly on Joe's left shoulder and says, "Joe, beware: devil woman! Awk!"

"You're right, Herbie. Enough games!" Joe has *shingen*, a high level of universal perspective that was taught to him by his sensei, Musashi, who once said, "Society must be protected."

As Joe unsheathes his sword, Ruth is sneaking up on Joe from the dark, but the dying war veteran, who is lying on the floor, wraps his arms tightly around one of her legs. "I bite too, *bitch!*" he says, sinking his teeth into Ruth's ankle.

"Aurh!" Ruth screams. Then she grabs the veteran's head violently. *Snap!* Ruth breaks the veteran's neck. Joe spins around, swinging his sword horizontally, slicing off both of Ruth's legs with one smooth samurai swing of his "archangel of honor" holy sword.

Joe shouts, *"Ashi!"* Ruth starts squirming toward Joe like a snake, and tries to bite him. He goes to one knee and does a *hidari gyaku kesa*, a two-handed cut, swinging his sword upward as if swinging for a home run. The blade lops off Ruth's head, which flies away and flops into the big bowl of fondue. *Swoosh!* The fondue splashes all over the men and women at the table.

Joe sheathes his sword. "The morning light will be here soon, but right now it's Halloween night!" Joe says. He and Herbie leave to patrol a residential Asian neighborhood.

It is Halloween night in an Asian neighborhood. As Joe and Herbie patrol, Joe says, "My sixth sense feels someone evil watching me."

"Don't worry, Joe. Irk!" says Herbie. They observe a pair of parents of Asian descent leaving a house. These people are going out to party at the trendy new dance club in Beverly Hills called Club Saman, leaving their young son, Bao, at home. Bao is around five years old, with relatives to babysit him. He is waiting for his other cousins to arrive, eating cookies and drinking milk in the kitchen. "Mm, good cookies," Bao says, while he reads Confucius. "I feel harmony!" Bao says.

He hears his young cousins arrive. They are left by Bao's uncles and aunts. "Let's party!" the parents say, as they were also invited to celebrate, receiving free tickets in the mail to attend Club Saman on Halloween night. Bao goes into the next room, where his cousins begin watching a funny movie on television. It's about a fat magic genie who is taking Aladdin on a carpet ride throughout Baghdad. Bao sits down on the carpet near the television with four of his young cousins. The two babysitting cousins are around fifteen years old. All of the adults have left the house on this Halloween night to go to an adults-only party at Club Saman. Bao feels happy, watching the very funny movie about a hilarious genie, and laughs with his cousins. Suddenly, in his peripheral vision, he sees someone looking at him. He looks to his left, where the front door is. The front door is mostly glass in the middle, with slender wood trim on the edges. It enables one to see the entire body of a person standing outside the front door. Bao sees a large scaly creature with horns and red eyes looking straight at him, as if looking inside him. Bao, extremely scared, feels his heart pounding hard. The evil-looking creature continues looking at him, sending telepathic messages to Bao's mind, "My name is Molech! It's Halloween. Come outside with me!" Scripture mentions Molech in Jeremiah 32:35.

Bao, out of breath, cannot bring himself to tell his cousins what is transpiring. His cousins are laughing at the comedy. Bao closes his eyes and then reopens them slowly in fear. He looks at the front door and sees nothing. He starts panicking and tells his one of his older cousins, who takes him to the kitchen with the other older female cousin named Cha, who says, "Calm down, Bao. Don't worry."

They try to calm Bao down, but finding themselves unable to do so, they take him outside, where they frightfully observe the shadowy image of a huge husky scaly serpent-looking man running across the street shouting, "Sacrilege!" He's being chased by an athletic young man, wielding a beautiful sword, with a parrot on his left shoulder.

Bao says, "Joe. That's Joe!" Everyone knows the Olympic champion fencer who is also the community reformer."

Bao hears the parrot shout, "Scare kids. Coward! Awk! Fool, stop! Face Joe!"

Herbie and Joe chase the demon Molech on Halloween night. Molech jumps into a deep hole in the ground that goes to the abyss. Joe says, "He disappeared, Herbie. I feel like going down there after him. And I feel my mortality too."

"Not now, Joe. One day ... with thy Father! Awk!" Joe is grateful for Herbie, who mysteriously, at times, has celestial advice. Joe walks back to the boys and girl to console them. The older cousins pick up Bao, and sit with the young boy on a fence post in the front yard as Joe arrives.

Joe says, "Do not be afraid of anything. Fear robs you of *hei-joshin*, prevents you from thinking clearly, and keeps you from reacting normally." Joe points up to the stars and calms Bao by telling him a story about the firmament.

One of Bao's older cousins says, *"Shh. Listen to Joe."* Everyone is amazed at Joe's storytelling. The story came from Joe's grandfather General Benson. Joe says, "I will tell you a story, just as my grandfather told me, when I was a child like you, Bao. I was camping in the mountains with my grandfather, who was a great leader and soldier."

Herbie, filled with anxiety, says, "Hurry, Joe. Irk!" Everyone laughs at Herbie.

Joe says, "Bao, look up at the stars and the moon. The Great Divine made these. The Great Divine Creator is the light, the bright good energy or Holy Spirit—God. And the dark has no light. The dark force of energy is bad or evil—which is always lurking nearby." Just then a huge ugly albatross lofts onto a neighbor's fence nearby, leering at Bao. Bao sees it. He starts to hyperventilate. Joe, the warrior and angel, says, "But in the night, Bao, when you look at the stars, or the moon, good divinity is with you, little brother. So calm down; it's okay."

Herbie says to the albatross, "Want a piece of me? Awk!" The albatross's eyes become huge as it spews foam from its mouth. Then it flies away. Bao stops hyperventilating, and with time calms down.

Shortly, the parents of all the children arrive from their Halloween party at Club Saman. They all wave good-bye to Joe. "Thanks, Joe!"

"You're welcome," Joe says. He walks gracefully down the block, heading back to Benson Manor for a quick bite to eat.

Herbie says, "Food, Joe. … Ark!" Herbie is happy and begins whistling a parrot tune.

After Joe is out of sight, Bao begins feeling uneasy again. Somehow, Bao's parents seem different. Bao says, "What is that little glow thing on your right hand, Daddy, Momma?"

Bao's dad and mom, with tears in their eyes, look at their right hands, which are marked and have a new glowing red human chip implant. Then, each with a devious smile, they say, "It's Halloween night!"

A little later that Halloween night, in Beverly Hills, at Benson Manor, Joe is lying on his bed, recuperating before he goes outside to make his final security rounds on this long Halloween night. He is resting his upper body while lying halfway off his bed, doing stomach crunches. Joe has his shirt off, so he can see his ripped stomach muscles flexing as he does the stomach crunches. Feeling that he has done enough stomach crunches, Joe says, "Feels good. And now to give my brain increased health!" Joe now moves his forehead off the edge of the bed, keeping his face tilted up toward the ceiling, away from the bed. He closes his eyes, and breathes air deep inside his lungs, allowing the majority of the blood to circulate through his brain, cleansing it, and nourishing it with nutrients. Joe remembers watching his late father, Dr. Robert Benson, doing this. He adopted the technique into his arsenal of exercises to improve his brain health.

Herbie mimics Joe, as parrots are wont do, and gets next to his master. He places his bird head so it tilts downward, facing the ground, to emulate Joe. Herbie closes his eyes. "This is the life!" he squawks. Joe spots what looks like a six-pack of abdominals on Herbie's stomach. Herbie sees this and says, "Stomach crunches, Joe. Awk!"

"What? Looks more like birdseed bulges of fine living," Joe says, laughing as he takes a closer look at Herbie's little abdomen.

In the near distance, beautiful music is being played on the grand piano by Rose. Joe listens, enjoying the moment. His room looks like this: On a high redwood rack on the wall is Joe's holy sword, unsheathed, with the inscription, "Joe, Archangel of Honor." Below the sword is a solid rectangular block pure ruby, which is the length of the sword and which rests on the ground. In the center of this this ruby stone lies a large Holy Bible. To the left of the Holy Bible is a photo of Joe and his fencing teacher, Napoleon. To the right side of the Bible is a photo of Joe and the late Sensei Musashi. A few feet in front of the Bible is a small table made from pure marble, with a priceless porcelain bowl atop it, given to Joe by Sensei Musashi. In the bowl is a variety of mixed nuts and seeds: pumpkin seeds, almonds, sunflower seeds, cashews, peanuts, and walnuts. Of course, next to Joe's bed are photos of his father and mother, along with a photo of Joe fishing with his grandfather. Joe knows his life on earth has purpose. As a man, he can blend into society to help people discover their perplexing needs. Joe has two roles on earth: one, as a royal knight for the king of England, and two, as God's human archangel of honor to help suppress evil.

Approximately a half hour goes by as Joe relaxingly allows blood flow to his head. He gets up and says, "My mind feels great!"

Herbie, also getting up, says, "Herbie's mind great, ark!" Herbie jumps on Joe's shoulder to hitch a ride as Joe walks toward the Holy Bible. Joe picks up the Holy Bible and reads, "Do not practice sacrifice! Do not practice black magic, voodoo, or call for evil spirits for aid! Do not practice evil worship or partake in evil celebrations of any kind or call for serpent charmers, mediums, wizards or spirits of the dead" (Deuteronomy 18:10–11)!

Joe takes a breath and continues. "These practices are sacrilege that will abolish you from a joyful eternal life in heaven with God" (Deuteronomy 18:12). He puts the Holy Bible down on its shelf and then grabs a handful of mixed nuts and seeds to eat. He also gives some to Herbie. Just then,

Rose walks into the room and says, "Joe! Why have you not answered your cell phone? Is it turned off?"

Joe, astonished, looks at his cell phone and says, "Yes, it's turned off. But how?"

Herbie, shaking his parrot head, says, "How? Who? Awk!"

Rose ponders a bit and then says, "Well, Joe, who are you? Charlotte has been trying to get in touch with you all night."

Joe looks at innocent Herbie and says, "I think I know who the who is!" Joe turns his cell phone on and sees a text from his old teacher and friend Napoleon. It reads, "Joe, may we see you this Halloween week in Mexico?" Joe wonders what Napoleon wants, but he chooses to immediately call his fiancée, Charlotte, instead. Joe pushes one button to automatically connect to his fiancée. "Charlotte, how are you? I miss you."

Charlotte says, "I don't like Halloween. It's scary, isn't it, Joe? I wish I were with you, Joe. What are you thinking about at this moment? And Joe, please be truthful and tell me what you are feeling at this moment."

Joe continues to talk to Charlotte, wondering why Charlotte is fishing his mind for his thoughts and feelings about Halloween night.

Herbie, thinking too, tilts his parrot head and then chirps, "Awk! Be careful, Joe. Remember Samson and Delilah!" Herbie then flies off with Rose to another part of the house.

Joe laughs. Then he says, "Well, I'm thinking, I miss Charlotte! Don't worry, I'm not scared of Halloween night."

"Hmm," she says. Then she places Joe on hold for about

fifteen seconds without letting him know beforehand. Joe begins to wonder if Charlotte is consoling someone. "I'm back, Joe. Sorry, darling! I feel like cuddling with you, my love. Are you leaving your safe home and going someplace on this frightening and dangerous Halloween night, Joe?"

"Leaving? Well, I don't know, Charlotte. Anything is possible. We are many miles of land apart, and an ocean away, which makes it impossible for us to cuddle, my sweet Charlotte. May I read you a prayer?" Joe says.

Charlotte warmly laughs with a hint of mystery. She says, "Yes, Joe! Say your prayers!"

Joe remains home for the last few hours of Halloween night, reading scriptures to his beloved fiancée, Charlotte.

The next morning comes early in Sonora, Mexico, at a place called Pueblo de Iglesia, where many locals build shrines with skulls to honor their dead relatives. This is in preparation for celebrating Día de los Muertos. Where Halloween ends, Día de los Muertos begins, and somehow the two are connected. In Pueblo de Iglesia, Lumbra drives her Mercedes sport utility vehicle hard, splashing through mudholes, going through narrow paths, and zooming along downhill slopes at an angle, while Napoleon's hands become white-knuckled, gripping the interior of the car for dear life. Lumbra's Mercedes SUV flies off the ground after going through huge dips in the road. They quickly arrive in town, with clay dust in the air behind them. Lumbra's first desire while they are there is to build a shrine on the grave of her *abuelos* (grandparents). Lumbra says, "I remember things here, Napoleon. *Yo tengo recuerdos, amor.*" (I have memories, my love.)

Napoleon says, "Memories are good, *ma chérie.*"

"*Sí, pero mi papa nunca gusto este lugar. No se porque.*" (Yes, but my father never liked this place. I don't know why.)

Napoleon laughs, and says, "*C'est la vie!*" (That's life!)

"Por fin llegamos, amor." (Finally we've arrived, my love.) Lumbra parks her SUV next to the cemetery. Many Mexican citizens are constructing shrines, using skulls that appear to be human.

Napoleon gets an eerie feeling. He worries about Joe, hoping he is fine. Napoleon says, "Lumbra, I have been texting Joe for days, but I've gotten no reply." Napoleon and Lumbra shrug their shoulders, hoping Joe is fine. Napoleon then helps his wife, Lumbra, remove things from the SUV and place them near Lumbra's grandparents' gravesite. He says, "I think I know why your father was uncomfortable being in this place. Let's finish up, yes?"

Lumbra looks at Napoleon and laughs. *"Tienes miedo, amor?"* (Are you afraid, my love?)

Napoleon responds, *"Je? En aucune facon!"* (Me? No way!)

On the gravesite, Lumbra places photos of her deceased grandparents, lighted candles with burning incense, and food, among other things. Then she begins building a shrine to honor her grandparents' time on earth, in honor Día de los Muertos (Day of the Dead).

Napoleon participates too. Taking a human skull out of the box of the dead grandparents' belongings, he nervously looks at Lumbra.

"No, silly, that is made out of wood." Lumbra laughs.

"Yes, I knew that. I am French, no? Hey, let's call Joe and ask him to visit us, yes?"

"Sí, mi amor." (Yes, my love) Lumbra approves of inviting Joe.

Napoleon says, "Where will we sleep tonight?"

Lumbra says, *"Dormir? No vamos a dormir."* (Sleep? We are not going to sleep.) She continues, "We are going to listen to stories, eat, drink, and hear guitar music all night long, mi amor."

Napoleon responds, *"C'est fine, mon amour."* (That's fine my love.)

On another gravesite, just a few gravestones away, a huge jolly Hispanic man starts playing his guitar while singing "La Vida y Muerto" (Life and Death). Napoleon, uneasy, opens his phone and dials Joe's cell phone number. Napoleon says, "Hi, Joe. You come down here to Mexico, my friend, yes!"

"Mexico? Hmm … sure, Napoleon!" Joe says. It's still early morning. Napoleon and Joe work out the flight arrangements, and Joe agrees he will arrive tonight. Napoleon says, *"Oui! Oui!"* (Yes! Yes!) Then he slaps his cupped hand over his mouth. *Pop!*

Finally, with effort, Lumbra and Napoleon finish building the shrine to honor Lumbra's dead abuelos. Then they start eating tamales, *posole, frijoles,* and *pan de los muertos,* the last of which is bread with sugar that is shaped to resemble human skulls. They and the people they're eating with all enjoy the fine food with music being played. Two señoras begin passing out handmade clay cups to everyone. Then the two señoras, who are very lovely, place four one-gallon jugs, each containing a gallon of pulque (agave-based liquor), in the center of the floor on top of a *lana* (wool) blanket. A sudden mysterious cold wind blows by as a man approximately ninety-nine years old walks into the area. He says, *"Por favor tomar, porque te vas a necesitar!"* (Please drink, because you will need it!)

Lumbra pours pulque into two cups, one for Napoleon and one for her. *"Napoleon, mi amor, escuchar al viejo,"* she says, advising her lover to listen to the old man.

The old man says, *"Salud! Prepararse, y escuchar una sincero viejo cuento de antes."* (Cheers! Prepare yourself, and listen to this old truthful story of the past.) The sun goes down; only the dark and a whistling cool wind remains. Everyone, including Lumbra and Napoleon, drinks a small cup of pulque, the two lovers wondering where Joe is.

"Here I am!" Joe says. Lumbra and Napoleon hug their friend

Joe, while Herbie jumps from shoulder to shoulder, saying hi to everyone in his own way. Joe and Herbie refuse a cup of pulque, but they do eat tamales with frijoles as they ready themselves for the old man's story. The old man looks left and then right, and begins telling the story of the wailing woman on this very dark night.

"Once upon a time, a Spanish soldier sailed from Spain on a mission to Mexico. Once he reached Mexico, he fell in love with a beautiful dark-skinned native woman. They had two children, whom the soldier loved very much. The soldier came from a rich family in Spain. His parents and friends disapproved of his mistress, threatening to disown him, or slay his children, if he refused to marry a Spanish woman from another rich family with whom they'd arranged the marriage. Not wishing to lose his inheritance, and hoping to spare his children, the soldier hid away his native mistress, who became his secretly kept woman, and sent for the woman from Spain, whom he did not know or love, to marry. The woman from Spain arrived a few days before Halloween. The marriage was set for Halloween night. As Halloween approached, the soldier's mistress was filled with a terrible jealous rage. She walked with her two children along the coast to church to witness her man, a handsome conquistador, marry the woman from Spain. She stood outside the church holding the hands of her children while crying, because she was not allowed inside, and desperately tried to stop the marriage. The children saw their father and cried, 'Papa!' He looked at his two children, but then he turned away, continuing with the ceremony until it was over and he was married to the woman from Spain. To avenge herself of having been betrayed by her unfaithful husband, the mistress drowned their two children in the ocean. The children pleaded, 'Why, Mama? No, Mama! Papa! Papa!' The soldier was horrified and broke down in tears when he heard what she had done with his adored children. He immediately thought of killing her, but instead he tried to have her arrested. The local authorities had no witnesses to the crime, and anyway they did not like the man from Spain, because they believed he abandoned his family, causing the horrific outcome. The soldier from Spain had all the money he would ever need thanks to having followed through with the arranged marriage. But the money did not matter to him anymore. He took a large sum of his ill-gained money and went to the local cantina that overlooked the ocean his children had been drowned in. He drank an enormous amounts of liquor there, thinking of his children. A few days passed. He died of alcohol poisoning. The ocean air blew across his foul, fermented dead body. The native woman, his first wife, the mother of the two children she drowned, driven insane by rage, jealousy, and guilt, traveled into the wild. She roamed through the land, searching the waterways for her children. But she could not find them. She traveled to various towns, and deliriously tried to grab other children away from their parents. She was driven away from each town with a fierce beating from the mothers. Finally, in agony in both body and mind, she drowned herself in the ocean. But the woman's spirit could not escape to heaven because of the weight of her terrible crimes, which included her suicide, which is against the laws of God. The spirit of la llorona, the wailing woman (Jeremiah 9:17), still wanders the earth. Especially on Halloween night, she walks searching for children through cemeteries, coastlines, riverbeds, lakes, and the wilderness, wailing in guilt and grief. She is condemned forever to search in vain for her children. But she will never find them, because they are no more. She might attempt to get your children on Halloween night in her effort to beguile God into thinking she has retrieved her drowned children, which is something that Satan recommended she do."

Having concluded the story of the wailing woman, the old man says one final thing: "Tonight has awakened those who were sleeping. Be aware. And come back next year. I have a secret about myself that I must unburden myself of."

As the winds whistle sounds through the trees, Lumbra says, "*Tienes sueno, mi amor? Quieres dormir?*" (Are you sleepy, my love? Do you want to sleep?) She shows Napoleon some wool blankets.

"Oui! But I am French, so I will wait for the sun to come up!" Napoleon says. Then he slaps his cupped hand over his puckered mouth: *pop!* Suddenly, Napoleon sees a shadowy figure walking toward him. He drinks two large swallows of pulque, lifting the gallon jug high to his lips.

The shadowy figure turns out to be the very old man, who crouches down, smiles with teeth of gold, and says, "Pour me a cup, *joven*." Joe, Lumbra, and Herbie laugh.

CHAPTER 6

The next day, everyone is very tired—Lumbra, Napoleon, Joe, and Herbie too. Napoleon makes a quality breakfast of ostrich eggs mixed with large green cactus leaves, also preparing fresh-squeezed red cactus pear juice to drink, with a spoon of agave nectar to sweeten it. Napoleon says, "Bon appétit!" Then he slaps his cupped hand over his mouth. *Pop!*

Lumbra says, *"Gracias, mi amor. Que te paracer, Joe?"* (Thank you, my love. What do you think, Joe?)

Joe, thankful, says, *"Gracias para desayuno, Napoleon y Lumbra."* (Thank you for the breakfast, Napoleon and Lumbra.) Herbie just nods his head in approval while he stuffs his parrot face. After breakfast, Lumbra teaches Joe more about how to decipher ancient codes using a book that once belonged to her late father. In the past, Lumbra often taught the curious Joe how to read ancient languages and hieroglyphs.

After a teaching lesson, they all walk over to the old bullring arena to watch a bullfight. Napoleon says, "I must show you a lesson, Joe—how to use your sword and kill a powerful beast with one single thrust! Yes!" Napoleon slaps his cupped hand over his mouth. *Pop!*

"Thank you, Napoleon. You will always be my great fencing teacher, and like a father to me," Joe says. He remembers his other swordplay teacher, Sensei Musashi, saying, "Thirst, Joe. A samurai must always thirst for knowledge, no matter how brutal it may be!"

As Joe, Lumbra, and Napoleon take their seats, Spanish music is played with trumpets and the matadors come into the bullring.

Lumbra says, "We only have time to see one bullfight." The first bullfight begins after a sole matador enters the bullring and takes his stylish black sombrero off to salute the crowd. Then, the huge bull enters the ring, charging the matador. As the bull passes him, the matador sticks his sword between the bull's shoulder blades, which causes the bull to bleed.

The bull gets wise, and focuses his horns on the sword. *Pop!* The bull knocks the matador's sword out of his hands. It falls to the ground. As the matador scrambles for his sword, the bull gouges the matador in his ribs. *"Augh!"* the matador screams. The bull chases the matador, running around him. The matador refuses help from other matadors, and the emergency ambulance that wants to take him to the hospital. The matador, with courage, while bleeding profusely from his ribs, finally retrieves his sword. Then he hides his sword in his red cape, holding it horizontally. The bull charges the red cape, and does not see the sword. With patience, the matador, after keeping his sword hidden behind the red cape, raises his sword above the charging bull. The crowd shouts, "Olé! Olé! Olé!" The matador and bull go through the same routine several times.

Herbie cries "Oh no! Oh no! Oh no!" He dives underneath Joe's shirt to hide.

The matador focuses on the bull's final charge. The bull's nostrils spew mucus and steam. The bull closes the gap between itself and the matador, enough for the matador to smell the bull's grassy breath. The matador quickly removes his sword from concealment and raises it, the sword's tip held at a special downward angle toward the bull's heart, to do a single sword thrust, which is called *estocada.* He plunges his sword deep into the bull's chest, stopping it in its tracks. The bull falls to the ground, dead. *Thump!*

Napoleon, chomping on pork rinds with salsa and lemon juice, says, "See, Joe? Did you see that technique? That's how you kill a beast!"

Joe concurs. "Yes. I saw how, Napoleon. It was the angle of the sword and the smooth delivery of the matador." They discuss how the matador plunged his sword at a special angle to kill the huge creature. Joe has just received another lesson of swordplay from his great fencing teacher Napoleon.

Lumbra says, "Hey, there's Chico, my cousin. He is near the ring where the matador dropped his red cape." She observes Chico reach in the bullring and grab the matador's red cape for a souvenir. Lumbra breaks up Joe and Napoleon's swordplay conversation and says, *"Los vamos!"* (Let's go!)

Napoleon says, "Oui, oui, ma chérie." (Yes, yes, my darling.) Emotional, they all walk out of the stadium, although there are still upcoming bullfights. They meet their tour guide and Lumbra's cousin Chico. Lumbra says, *"Hola, Chico, mi primo favorite!"* (Hello Chico, my favorite cousin!)

The middle-aged man says, *"Hola, mi prima!"* (Hello, my cousin!) Chico shakes Joe's and Napoleon's hands and slaps Herbie lightly across his beak. Chico says, "My real name is Cherio, but starting when I was a little boy, everybody called me Chico. The name stuck!" He laughs.

Herbie shouts, "Cheerios! Cheerios! Awk."

Then Lumbra gives everyone the eye. They all know there is work to do. They all get into Lumbra's Mercedes SUV. Since Lumbra has a goal in life that she pursues with determination and enthusiasm, she says, "Go, Chico! Drive."

"Yes, Cousin." Chico vigorously drives them down various roads for miles, following the road map Lumbra had highlighted for him. They finally reach the place for their archeological expedition: an Aztec pyramid in the unexplored jungles near Mexico City. Chico says, "We're here, my friends." They all exit the vehicle.

Lumbra, after reviewing the old map of her father, says, "There must be an opening around the eye symbol. That's what the hieroglyph says. Then, as Lumbra feels with her hands, *boom!* A trapdoor opens that leads down a narrow passage.

Chico wraps his red cape around his body—"For good luck," he mentions. Then they all walk down the narrow passage, following Lumbra, with Napoleon close by her side. Lumbra shines her handheld high-powered spotlight to see as they walk downward. The air begins to get musty as they go deeper and deeper. After walking 6,666 meters, they finally reach an opening. They hear water and see a cenote, which is freshwater pool that has been meticulously filtered by the earth. The water is so clear that they can see small fish frolicking amid the plant life. Lumbra says, "This water has vitamin- and mineral-rich algae that nourish and protect your skin. Possibly it is the Fountain of Youth." Chico takes a quick bath while Napoleon drinks down gulps of water.

Lumbra and Joe study the huge underground cave wall's hieroglyphs below the pyramid. Joe says, "Hmm," with Herbie perched on his left shoulder. Then Joe places his strong right hand on the handle of his sword, ready to pull it out. Joe's sixth sense feels danger. With his good eyesight, he scans the area. He says, "Fly up and around, Herbie, please." Herbie soars high up in the air.

After drinking plenty of water, Napoleon helps his wife, Lumbra, with her archeological equipment. Lumbra uses her steel chisel to dig near a symbol, what looks like a carving of a huge beast. The curves of Lumbra's body are amplified by the small sexy outfit she is wearing. Both she and Napoleon, the latter of whom is enjoying a body rejuvenated by minerals, discover a box made of petrified wood. Napoleon, Chico, and Joe do not understand the writing on the box, but Lumbra does. She says, "It's the ancient Nahuatl language of the Mesoamerican people. It reads, 'Book of Knowledge'!" Joe opens the sealed box with his sword. Lumbra takes out the Book of Knowledge, the lost Book of Itzamna.

Napoleon says, "It's hard for me to concentrate on the book, Lumbra. My heart has eyes only for you, ma chérie!" *Pop!* Napoleon slaps his puckered mouth and then continues. "Kiss! Kiss! You, my wife, are now an accomplished swordswoman, yes?" Napoleon says.

Lumbra says, "I say yes, mi amor!" For a brief moment, they kiss deeply while caressing each other's bodies, enjoying their moment of lovemaking to their hearts' satisfaction. Lumbra sees it as a victory that she has finally acquired the Book of Knowledge, something her father had looked for years ago.

Lumbra is a dedicated archeologist and a nurse who has become an athlete with all the climbing, digging, and lovemaking she's done with her French husband, Napoleon. Napoleon has always been an athlete. He won a silver medal at the Olympic Games held in France years ago.

Joe, with Herbie on his shoulder, says, "Way to go!" He smiles and gives the two-thumbs-up signal.

As they group begin to walk toward the passage from whence they came to exit, it crumbles, boulders sealing it shut.

"Oh no!" cries Lumbra. Napoleon, Chico, and Joe shake their heads.

Herbie says, "Over there, Joe. Awk."

"Let's follow Herbie," Joe says. As Herbie flies forward, they walk behind him. They walk into another opening, which looks like an underground bullring.

Chico says, "There must have been a matador here in the ancient past." Looking around, they see remnants of bones, people, and beasts. *Rrrr!* Screams come from nearby.

Then everyone sees a huge *Tyrannosaurus rex* coming at them. *"Augh!"* they all scream, except for Joe, whose adrenaline, released because death is in the air, makes his heart pound.

Joe says, "Calm down." He thrusts his sword into the T. rex's shoulder. *Stab!* The T. rex groans. It almost grabs Joe's sword with its huge dinosaur mouth. The T. rex begins to focus its killer hunting ability on Joe, but Herbie, sensing this, swoops into the T. rex's eye, clawing and pecking. The dinosaur swivels its head in a repeated circular motion and uses its bottom jaw to knock Herbie to the ground. Herbie flops onto the ground, helpless as the dinosaur's mouth opens, saliva dripping from its teeth and dropping onto Herbie. "No! I lost you once, Herbie. That won't happen again," Joe says. He starts slashing the dinosaur's side. *Slash! Slash!* The T. rex instinctively swings its huge tail, whipping Joe in his belly. *"Augh!"* Joe cries, dropping his sword and falling backward. Joe, on the ground, with blood spilling out his mouth, has internal damage. Yet, as a warrior, Joe breathes in puffs of air, a technique his sensei, Musashi, taught him. He regains his composure as the dinosaur comes after him. Once the T. rex is close enough, Joe does a martial arts forward roll, almost as a round tire, and rolls underneath the dinosaur, between its legs. Now that Joe is behind the dinosaur, he runs and grabs his sword with one hand and picks up Herbie with his other hand. Joe quickly gives Herbie to Chico.

Herbie says, "Hide sword, Joe. Awk."

Chico tosses his red matador cape at Joe and says, "Matador Joe. You are the matador!"

Napoleon shouts, "Yes, Joe! Remember the bullfight. You can do it, my son." Napoleon cups his hand to slap his mouth. *Pop!* Joe positions himself in the fencing en garde positon. The huge T. rex growls. *Aar!* Then it charges Joe, who hides his sword inside the red cape. The charging dinosaur has two horns on its head. It passes by several times, almost spearing Joe, attempting to kill Joe.

"*Olé! Olé! Olé!*" Chico, Napoleon, and Herbie shout.

Lumbra just hugs Napoleon. She says a prayer: "*Señor, por favor, ayudar nosotros!*" (Lord, please, help us!)

Joe now focuses his ki energy, saying, "God, help me kill this beast." The T. rex charges Joe, its mouth open, showing its powerful teeth. Joe shows the red cape, luring the beast. When the dinosaur is within striking range, Joe pulls out his sword and holds it at a horizontal angle, with the point slightly downward, facing the beast's heart. Joe plunges his celestial angel sword deep into the T. rex's chest, killing the beast instantly. *Kaboom!* The *Tyrannosaurus rex* falls hard to the ground.

Napoleon shouts with pride, "My Joe! You are my greatest student. My son Joe." Napoleon goes over and hugs Joe, as do with Herbie and Lumbra.

Chico nervously says, "*Necesito una cerveza!*" (I need a beer.)

Napoleon says, "Let's get out of here. I must see France again."

Joe is injured, but he hides his injury from his friends, who continue to follow Herbie. Going up a path toward the top, they see sunlight.

"Here! Awk," Herbie says.

Lumbra gets her shovel and steel digging pole. Chico and Napoleon use the tools to dig an opening, while Joe stays on guard for any trouble. Herbie, knowing Joe is injured, says, "Dig. Dig faster! Awk."

Chico says, "*Caramba, que un pajaro!*" (Wow, what a bird!)

As they dig to tunnel themselves out, someone is watching them from far away in a castle. It's Samara looking through her crystal ball, observing Lumbra, Napoleon, Chico, Joe, and Herbie. She caresses her familiar, saying, "Jezebel, my pretty. What have we got here?" Samara, devilishly excited, discovers that Lumbra has found the lost Book of Itzamna, the Book of Knowledge. Samara goes into a trance, her eyes bugging out and her body spinning. She slowly closes her eyes and then reopens them. Blood spills from her eyes while she chants in Latin, "*Da mihi in libro Itzamna!*" (Give me the Book of Itzamna!) The castle ground beneath Samara's feet trembles—*barump.*

Finally, as a team, the expeditioners make a big enough opening. Lumbra says, "Let's go!" She and the others climb out of the Aztec pyramid. Curious, they look inside the Book of Itzamna, and discover it has architecture and mathematical formulas with scientific principles that involve regenerated natural electricity. "How does this knowledge exist?" Lumbra shakes her head and says, "No one today has this type of knowledge!"

Napoleon says, "Why don't we take this book back to France, so a French scientist can decipher these formulas, ma chérie?"

Lumbra, initially quiet, soon says, "Maybe I should take this to the Mexican president and he can have a Mexican scientist decipher it."

"No, Cousin. Sell it!" says Chico.

Lumbra and Napoleon look at each other and say, "Joe, what do we do?"

Suddenly, a sandstorm strikes the area. They all start walking back to Lumbra's vehicle, staggering against the powerful wind to get there. Then, once at the vehicle, they discover ten Mexican bandito men wielding huge steel machetes. Joe shouts, "Quickly, run back to the pyramid!" Joe unsheathes his sword and holds it with both hands in front of him to protect the center of his body.

Joe opens his eyes wide, giving him a wider scope of peripheral vision with which to watch his opponents, as Herbie flies up in the sky and says, "Get them, Joe!" As the banditos rush Joe, he sidesteps to his left, keeping the big chunky bandito in front of him, which blocks out the other assailants. Joe swings his sword down diagonally, severing the big bandito's head and a piece of his shoulder, and then smoothly swings his sword upward at an angle, severing the shoulder of the next assailant wielding a machete. As the other banditos rush, Joe quickly swings his sword horizontally, lopping off three banditos' heads. Then he springs atop the SUV's hood. One of the five banditos remaining says, "*Cabron!*" (Dumbass!) Just then, Herbie drops some rocks from above. They hit two of the banditos.

"*Auh!*" they say. Joe does a spinning roundhouse heel kick from the hood of the car. His kick strikes the other three banditos in their jaws. *Crack! Crack! Crack!* They drop to the ground hard, their faces smacking the dirt. *Puff!*

Meanwhile, just several yards away, Chico pulls out his large machete. Lumbra and Napoleon desperately attempt to get inside the pyramid and hide. Three large muscular pig-faced men attempt to grab Lumbra and take the Book of Knowledge from her, but Chico strikes two of them in the neck. Greenish-purple blood spurts out. Then a previously unseen pig-faced midget sneaks up on Chico and thrusts a dagger into his spleen. As Chico screams in pain, four more pig-faced men punch and push Chico and Napoleon. As the pig-faced midget points his dagger at Lumbra, two huge pig-faced men grab her. Lumbra cries, "*Mi amor, ayudame!*" (My love, help me!) Napoleon breaks loose, and temporarily frees Lumbra. Chico, severely bleeding, gets pummeled and is knocked unconscious. Then Lumbra, desperate, grabs a machete from the ground and gets ready to fight.

Suddenly, a witch woman wearing a black cape appears standing on a big rock. The witch says, "I am the Great Witch!"

Napoleon shouts, "You are the *Great Bitch!*" Napoleon charges the witch, but a pig-faced man strikes him in the head with a human skull, knocking him unconscious. One pig-faced man attempts to grab Lumbra. She drops the Book of Knowledge and rushes to aid Napoleon, using her own machete to stab, slice, and sever head of the huge pig-faced man. *Plop!* The big pig man drops dead. Lumbra's fencing skills, taught to her by her husband, Napoleon, are deadly.

The pig-faced midget quickly retrieves the book off the ground and gives it to the Great Witch Samara, who hurriedly jumps into a dune buggy. Her pig-faced chauffeur drives the dune buggy erratically. Happily having gotten away with the Book of Knowledge, she shouts, *"A-ha-ha-ha!"*

The other banditos who were fighting Joe, keeping him busy, also scramble out of the area. They get into a four-wheel-drive passenger van, shouting, "Los vamos!"

Joe, staggering and spitting up blood, helps Lumbra get Napoleon and Chico into her vehicle. Herbie says, "Go! Doctor. Awk!"

"Yes, let's hurry! We all need a doctor," Joe says. Lumbra concurs. She speeds down the road to the nearest hospital, which is back at the pueblo. Chico looks out the car window and up to the clouds, saying his last dying words: *"Viva Dios! Sí, Gabriel, yo confío en Dios!"* Joe appreciates Chico's last words of faith in God.

His hands slightly shaking from loss of blood, Joe uses his cell phone. "Rose, I will be held up in Mexico for a while, helping friends. I will see you as soon as I can."

"Of course, Joe. And Joe, your fiancée, Charlotte, called me. I will be flying to England soon to help her. I love you, my brother! Don't worry, Joe. ... Good-bye," Rose says, feeling a little melancholy.

CHAPTER 7

Rose is thinking of a special man to whom she has become attracted this past Halloween week. And this man is in Bohemian Grove, Monte Rio, California, where a human sacrifice is taking place. There is a giant horned owl statue representing Molech that has huge hands with palms up and fire underneath to burn the victims. There are many leaders of the world, all men, there in attendance. One of the men attendees receives a phone call. "Yes, Rose. … Oh, Joe is away right now. Please don't worry. I am just a phone call away," the mysterious magnate says.

Suddenly, a voice shouts, "Please stop!" An individual, bound with ropes and screaming, is thrown into the huge statue's palms, which are filled with fire.

"*Aaaa!*" screams the sacrificial victim. All the leaders of many countries stand up, raise their right hands into the air, and press their two middle fingers into their palms, keeping extended their pinkies, index fingers, and thumbs, to display the sign of the horned owl (Molech). "*Novus Ordo Seclorum!*" all the leaders cheer.

Chapter 8

Sometime during this unholy Halloween week in Vatican City, the pope, head of the Roman Catholic Church, has a vision while he's asleep. The vision is of an angel instructing him to form a meeting of religious leaders from around the world. He is to have his two servants acquire a mysterious book possibly belonging to the ancient Maya, or Aztecs, which is hidden within the Vatican secret archives. This book has an inscription of the number 0 on it and describes in detail Halloween's mystery involving a possibly celestial fallen angel. The book must be opened only in front of the religious leaders, and then read for them all to hear so they can decide what to do.

The morning after his vision, the pope—or Papa, as the locals call him—gives his special messenger, a teenaged boy called Wheels, a briefcase filled with personal messages and some foul-smelling cempasuchil flowers. He is instructed to carry all the invitation messages and hand-deliver them to various religious leaders around the world. Wheels is an adopted orphan of the Catholic Church with a speech impediment, but he is very agile, known to spring up from the ground onto rooftops like a monkey. Some say he can run with the speed of a cheetah. Wheels will quite possibly represent the Vatican in the next Olympic Games.

Before Wheels departs the Vatican, he stops to say good-bye to his sweetheart, a teenaged girl named Angelina. Wheels walks into the cathedral slowly while Angelina plays harmonious music on the pipe organ, her long elegant fingers striking many keys, and her feet pumping the pedals. Wheels takes fresh-picked red roses from his briefcase and lays them on top of Angelina's organ. "I love you!" Wheels says.

Angelina cries and says, "Kiss me!" Wheels kisses Angelina on her full, warm, sweet lips, then looks deep into her eyes. It's their first love, teenage love. They are both sixteen years old.

Wheels sadly says, "I must secretly help the church and help the world. I love you, Angelina! I will see you soon. Good-bye, Angelina!"

Angelina cries and smiles. "I love you in this world, but you are of the other world, my love." Angelina continues crying as Wheels walks away. He slowly closes the huge castle doors behind him. *Kaboom!*

Wheels sighs as he gets into the Vatican's technologically advanced helicopter–jet airplane combination outside. The pilot's face is covered by a lifelike mask fashioned from jade, obsidian, and shells. His scary saucer eyes protrude from the mask. He wears this mask because he has a deformed face, the result of an accident involving Mother Superior Samara. "Hello, da Vinci! Let's rock and roll!" Wheels says. Da Vinci, saying nothing, immediately raises his hands and puts both thumbs up to signal a yes. Wheels feels like asking da Vinci where he got that ancient relic Maya mask made of jade, but da Vinci's scary saucer eyes frighten him. Da Vinci turns on the copter's radio to play a new type of music that seems to be a mixture of rock and roll and classical—not quite classical and not quite rock and roll, and very unusual. "Way to go, da Vinci! Hey, where does your family come from?" Wheels inquires.

"We da Vincis go way back in history," da Vinci says, as the aerodynamic chopper plane lifts off the ground and then shoots toward the sky. The aircraft is licensed to land anywhere in the world, whether the country is democratic, communist, capitalist, a dictatorship, or a monarchy, or even if anarchy reigns there.

Angelina, still crying and thinking of Wheels, continues playing the huge pipe organ precariously, as henchmen followers wearing dark hoods over their faces surround her. Above Angelina, Mother Superior Samara gazes at her from the balcony, and says, "She will do!" Then the henchmen, grunting with pig sounds—*Oink! Oink!*—subdue Angelina and whisk her away.

Wheels's cell phone rings and then stops. It was a call from his sweetheart, Angelina. Wheels calls her back, only to get a busy signal. "Hmm," Wheels says. Observing what has transpired, da Vinci's saucer eyes look worried. He reaches out with his hand and squeezes Wheels's arm gently. Da Vinci's voice sounds like an electronic robot recording as he says, "I know what happened. I will tell you!" Immediately Wheels breaks out crying. Da Vinci informs him of Samara. Nevertheless, Wheels must continue on his mission to help the papa.

The aircraft soars through the air at the speed of sound. All countries on earth clear this Vatican aircraft for landing at any time of day or year.

Wheels begins in Europe by personally giving an invitation, accompanied by a cempasuchil flower, to religious leaders such as padres, monks, and ministers, requesting that they arrive in Rome to attend a special meeting hosted by the pope. As the religious leaders receive the foul-smelling cempasuchil flowers, their eyes open wide with horror. Then they see a small note attached to the flower. They read this secret note, which is respectfully requesting their presence at an important meeting. They look for the messenger Wheels, but he is gone with the wind—as he can run with the speed of a cheetah.

CHAPTER 9

Several weeks have passed since Halloween week, thus allowing the pope time to ensure the presence of various world religious leaders. They are to attend a meeting, as instructed by a divinity claiming to be the angel named Gabriel, who appeared in the pope's dream. Joe was also called, by the king of England, to attend the secret meeting at the Vatican, where the pope has requested the king's best knight: Joe! It's a meeting concerning mysterious Halloween and what can be done to inspire more faith in the world. The pope reads aloud from a mysterious ancient book that gives celestial instructions for what is to happen on Halloween.

At night, the pope gives each of his two young servants, Jerry and Dean, a travel bag. Each bag is filled with organic emergency medical supplies. Jerry and Dean bow down to the papa. Each kiss his hand, which has a noticeable Water Mason ring on the darkened, possibly dead, ring finger. As they turn to depart, Joe enters the room. The pope asks Joe to sit down for a briefing on Halloween's mission. Joe says to Jerry and Dean, "I'll meet up with you two guys later, right after I meet with the papa."

Herbie, perched on Joe's left shoulder, says, "Joe. You need Joe!"

"Okay, Joe!" say the pope's two young servants, laughing.

Jerry and Dean depart, walking down a dungeon and through a corridor toward the Vatican archives.

Frightened, Jerry and Dean observe a shadowy woman appear, seemingly out of nowhere. She walks her four huge Rottweilers by the two young servants. The dogs begin growling and licking their chops. Jerry seems a little frightened, but not Dean. "Excuse me, lady! You're not allowed to bring dogs into this area of the Vatican! Who in hell are you?" Dean sternly says. In his peripheral vision, he sees that the lady possibly has a sharp-bladed dagger in her possession.

"Dean, ignore her, whoever she is! I don't know why she covers her face with clothing, and I don't care. We have to find the Mayan book with the numeral 0 on the cover and then give it immediately to the papa!" Jerry says. Suddenly, the big Rottweilers bark viciously from a distance, scaring Jerry, causing him to fall down on the ground. *Thud!*

"Careful, man! Watch what you're doing, Jerry," Dean says. Hearing the big dogs making sniffing noises and growling, the two servants approach. The big dogs begin to chase Jerry and Dean. Jerry falls and is mauled by two of the Rottweilers. *"Auh!"* Dean quickly looks back in horror, then he closes the doors behind him and enters the Vatican archives vault. "I'm sure glad those dumb dogs can't open doors," Dean says. Dean now begins a systematic search of the archives, knowing that the book, mysteriously, is not in its assigned location

Dean finally locates the misplaced book within the Vatican archives, and puts it in his bag. He says to himself, "Hey, look here, there's one book with a cover reading, 'Vicarius Filii Dei.' It seems to have information about the papa, and all Catholic priests who have passed. I wonder if the apostle Peter was truly the first papa." As Dean starts flipping through the pages, a woman's hand grabs the book out of his hands. He looks and sees a mysterious woman with a veil covering her face. He shouts, "Hey, stop, lady! You're not supposed to take archives out of here without permission."

She curtly says, "I gave myself permission!" Then she stabs her dagger deep into Dean's chest. Blood spurts out profusely as Dean falls to the ground. Then the woman slithers away, laughing as Dean lies bleeding in a pool of his own blood. Dean suddenly hears a violin being played—beautiful celestial music. He looks and sees a padre standing on an altar built from stone.

As the music fades and the padre mysteriously disappears, Dean says, "Need to get book to Papa." Dean, still bleeding, takes a small pouch from his bag. Then he takes a small jar from the pouch and opens it. He puts two fingers into the jar, takes out some clay ointment, and smears it on his punctured chest to slow the bleeding. Then he says, "Good." Dean then takes a miniature glass vial from the pouch, opens the cap, and drinks down the green liquid. He says, "Mm. I forget what plant this is made from, but my body feels warm." Dean, instantly rejuvenated, gets up from the floor and walks out the back door of the vault, away from the dogs.

No one is certain why the book that Dean was after was always misplaced. It's as if it has legs to walk around, or perhaps someone within the Vatican has been reading it.

Dean hears a heavy door opening ahead. It's Joe, with Herbie on his left shoulder. "Help me, Joe!"

"Dean, you're bleeding!"

"Yes, Joe, but I must take this bag to the papa. It contains a book with ancient encryption. This book must reach the papa!" Joe's sixth sense tells him that danger is near. Suddenly, with beastly speed, the four big Rottweilers pounce on Joe and Dean. As the vicious dogs snap their big teeth at Joe and Dean, violin music starts up nearby. The big dogs stop barking and are somehow distracted as Joe and Dean scramble for the exit. The music stops. The big dogs begin pursuit again, and gain on Joe and Dean.

Herbie suggests, "Fight them, Joe!"

Quickly and fluidly, Joe takes his sword from its scabbard and says, "Keep running, Dean!" Dean acknowledges and continues running, holding his bag like a football. Joe assumes a fighting stance, with his holy sword held out in front of his body. The four huge dogs, all teeth, are four feet away. Joe goes down on one knee and swings his sword horizontally—*whiff!*—decapitating the four big Rottweilers. As the dogs' heads bounce and roll on the ground, Joe angles his sword downward for a chiburi, flicking the blood to the ground. Taking a breath, Joe places his sword back into its scabbard. "Let's go, Herbie."

"Let's go, Joe."

Joe smoothly gets up to a standing position. Herbie kisses him on the face with his little black parrot tongue. Joe smiles, then walks gracefully away from the Vatican's archives area, feeding Herbie crackers over his left shoulder.

Herbie says, "Look, Joe. Ark!" Joe observes Dean crawling on the floor. Joe picks up Dean and slings him over his shoulder. "Follow, Joe!" Herbie says as he flies ahead to lead the way.

The huge Vatican bell rings, sending a message to the pope. Once Joe and Dean arrive at the pope's Vatican headquarters room, the pope says, "Please come in. I have been expecting you."

Dean says, "Let me down, Joe. Please." Joe smiles and removes Dean from his shoulders, gently placing Dean down in a standing position. "Thanks, Joe." Dean, in enormous pain, his chest pounding from the dagger puncture, staggers toward the papa to personally give him the ancient Maya book. Dean slowly takes the book out of his bag. He kisses the papa's hand. Then he gives the book to him and says, "*Princeps terrae, papa mea.*" (Earth's leader. My papa.) "I regret to inform you, someone stole a valuable book from the Vatican vault that has information about all Catholic popes." The papa's eyes open up big. Dean suddenly collapses, dead, falling into the papa's arms.

The next day, the pope gratefully addresses the religious leaders of the world. His purpose is to unite people of all religions, including Christianity (including Pentecostal, Orthodox, Lutheran, Baptist, and Seventh-Day Adventist), Hinduism, Islam, Judaism, Buddhism, Taoism, and many other religious faiths, representatives of which are seated in a large meeting room. Suddenly the meeting is interrupted by a newly promoted abbess named Samara, who is a strong female of high ranking. Samara demonstrates her poise and presence as she glares at all the men in the room. One religious leader says, "Why is this woman in here?"

The pope says, "Please quiet down, everybody. Samara, may I help you, my child?" Samara does not answer. She rolls her eyes up as she observes the mysterious Maya book in the pope's hands that appears to resemble the Voynich manuscript. Samara glares with her big shark eyes, smiles mischievously at everyone, and then quietly excuses herself. "Samara has given her whole life to the church. For this we must respect her. She is our esteemed abbess," the pope says, restoring order.

A magnate named Edward Bubo Dicaprio enters the room. The pope says, "Hello, Bubo! It's an honor for us to have your presence. Please come in. You are just in time. Gentleman, Bubo is a friend. Because the world is experiencing an economic downturn, he has been gracious enough to assist us in funding our interests, so long as our purpose intertwines with his."

"Hello, Papa!" says Bubo, kissing the pope's hand. Then Bubo gestures. "Good evening, gentlemen. I am the one who is esteemed by your presence." The magnate Bubo waves his hand, looking like a horned owl. Everyone stares at the eye-catching Water Mason ring on his finger. He sits down.

Now that everyone is poised, the pope tells the old story of how this Maya book first came into religious hands. The pope flashes back to Halloween in AD 1562, when Bishop Diego de Landa arrived in the Yucatán with Spanish warriors. They found approximately three hundred Mayas, and a young boy who was about to be sacrificed on a Mayan altar. Bishop Diego ran directly toward the boy as the latter was being cut with knives. The Spanish warriors ran with Bishop Diego and fought the Mayans as best they could. Finally Bishop Diego reached the young boy, who was being held down for sacrifice, and saved him, gathering him up into his arms. The young boy cried tears of relief. The Mayas who were not killed ran away, although some were captured for interrogation. The young boy's mother was located. The two cried after being reunited. Bishop Diego looked at the Maya structure and discerned the people's practice of astronomy. He wondered how they had come to be so advanced, and whose intelligence had helped them to achieve such celestial feats. He, along with some Spanish warriors, observed a vast Mayan library. He quickly spotted a book with inscribed with Maya number 0 and the distorted name Kukulkan. He looked inside the book, and his nerves went into shock. He immediately started praying to God, concealing the book under his robe so the other men would not see it. Bishop Diego then said, "There will be no more sacrifice here! Collect three books for saving, and auto-da-fé the rest immediately!" The remaining Mayan library, in its entirety, was burned to ashes.

The pope drinks a glass of tonic water and then begins reading from the book. The book informs the religious leaders of the demonic evil practice of sacrifice conducted around the world on Halloween in honor of a powerful fallen angel. There is a map inside the book giving directions to an island off the Yucatán that exists in the fifth dimension and appears every Halloween. There the religious leaders are to meet a person called Namas, who will supply the needed information regarding Halloween's mystery. This holy mission must be completed, or evil demonic spirits will flood the world with tragic chaos on Halloween. The book states that the fallen angel known as Kukulkan to the Maya was called Quetzalcoat by the Aztecs, and Supay by the Incas. The Incas created many designs visible from the sky by following the instructions of Supay, a flying serpent. The book states there is a Book of Knowledge that the fallen angel lost to a mortal, who then gave it to Saman for safekeeping. This Book of Knowledge provides guidance on how to achieve longevity when building such things as pyramids. The pope expresses his regret that his people have not yet discovered the whereabouts of the Book of Knowledge, but the pope hopes it was burned to ashes many years ago by Bishop Diego. The pope proclaims, "Then it is agreed to by all to abrogate Halloween!"

"Yes, Papa!" every religious leader concurs.

Taking a piece of paper from the book, the pope reads it, a note handwritten by Bishop Diego, which states, "Cast off the works of darkness and put on the amour of light" (Romans 13:12).

The religious leaders reply, "What does this mean?" The pope positions his miter, which has "Vicarius Filii Dei" embroidered on it, on his head and then says, "Novus Ordo Seclorum." With commanding presence, he continues: "I have summoned the king of England, who informs me that several royal knights, including the knight of honor, will go with the esteemed individuals of various religions I have selected. This prophecy, in the name of Jesus, will give us the armor of light."

The religious leaders all utter, "Who is this knight of honor?"

The pope confidently proclaims, "Joe!" Joe, holding a map of the area where the Halloween mission is to take place, enters the room, with Herbie on his left shoulder.

Joe, a vision of health and strength, proudly steps up to a podium to give a short speech. "We are here today as a team, as a family. Human beings of this world are wasting the short lives they have here on earth by judging others. Instead, every day they should be helping people they come across, and family. They should be loving one another instead of judging or ignoring people. People alive in this world should show love for one another." All of a sudden, all of the religious leaders get up from their chairs and start hugging one another, their tears flowing.

CHAPTER 10

A few days later, after Joe has been thoroughly briefed by the pope in private chambers regarding his upcoming dangerous mission involving the mystery of Halloween, Joe receives a pounding knock on his bedroom door at the Vatican. It's the messenger boy named Wheels, bringing him a plate of breakfast with hot coffee, and a sealed letter from the king of England. Wheels says, "I wish to help you, sir, ye royal knight, Joe!"

"Help me? Well, thank you," Joe says. Turning around, he grabs two silver coins from his travel bag, for a tip. But the boy has vanished, without a sound.

Herbie says, "He don't need wings, Joe. Fast! Ark!"

"You're not kidding, feathered friend. ... Hmm!" From the desk drawer, Joe grabs a letter opener made of human bone. He inserts the letter opener and flicks open the envelope. "It's the king, requesting my presence in England," says Joe.

Joe takes a deep sip of his deliciously strong-flavored cup of joe. Then, with the breakfast knife, he stabs into the Italian cheese, placing a slice between two pieces of fresh Italian bread. Joe eats while thinking deep. He contemplates how he can reach England in an expedient manner.

Herbie, flying above, alights onto Joe's left shoulder, holding Joe's US passport in his beak. Herbie says, "Let's fly, Joe. Irk!"

"Yes, Herbie. Vatican City is only twelve miles from Fiumicino Airport. Let's fly to England, my friend. But how did you know what I was thinking, Herbie?"

"I ear-hustle, Joe—ear-hustle. Awk!" Herbie replies. They both laugh.

Joe and Herbie get on an airplane, which is catered by a lovely stewardess named Kim. She spots Joe and says, "I see no ring on your finger, handsome. Does that mean you're free?"

"Everyone has free will, if that's what you mean, kind lady," Joe says.

"Joe's taken. Irk!" Herbie interrupts.

Just then, a man wearing a disguise on his face, slides a sword from underneath one of the airline seats. Evidently the sword had been planted there prior to the plane's boarding. "Okay, everybody! This is a hijack! And yes, stupid infidels, I'm a soldier of the New World Order! Listen up, stupid people! Who here is an American?" the hijacker man shouts, salivating.

Joe, with Herbie on his left shoulder, stands up and says, "I'm American, and proud of it!"

The hijacker looks furiously at Joe and shouts, "Come here, birdman! Now!"

Instantly, Joe feels the adrenaline rush of death in the air. He unsheathes his holy sword of honor and says, "Let's rock!"

"How did you get that sword through customs?" the baffled, angry hijacker shouts. Joe raises his sword high in the air, ready to attack.

Herbie, defending his friend, says to the hijacker, "How did you get through customs wearing that ugly face disguise? Awk!"

Furious, the hijacker's eyes light up with anger. He starts slashing at Herbie with his sword. Then Joe extends his sword with his strong hand, intending to intercept the hijacker's sword. *Clank!* Both blades connect to create a spark that causes a small fire thanks to the liquor on the liquor cart. The stewardess, Kim, grabs the emergency fire extinguisher. Herbie swoops down with parrot wings, and with his claws picks up a large pitcher of milk from the galley counter. Then he pours the milk on the fire, accidentally spilling some on some passengers.

"Auh!" the milk-wet passengers gripe.

Kim is a beautiful and intelligent stewardess—very professional. She and Herbie put out the fire while the hijacker and Joe square off. The hijacker is a highly trained swordsman, but he is no match for Joe, who is a master swordsman. The hijacker, in anger, strikes out at an innocent passenger to distract Joe. But Joe *tsuki* (thrusts) his sword forward, cutting the hijacker's arm. Then Joe, the Olympic fencing champion, strikes again with his sword, using a beat to make crisp contact with the hijacker's blade. He disarms the hijacker, whose sword falls to the ground. *Plunk!* Joe now smoothly places the point of his sword against the hijacker's chest. The hijacker's heart sounds loudly—*lub-dub, lub-dub, lub-dub*—and his eyes look like those of a frightened mouse. Joe focuses the point of his sword for the coup de grâce.

"Please do not kill me! I have thirteen children, and a parrot more handsome than yours," the hijacker says.

Suddenly, a man shouts orders. "Air marshal here!" The air marshal places handcuffs on the terrorist hijacker. Looking at Joe, he says, "I'll be back to talk you about that sword you have, Olympic fencing champ!" The air marshal briskly escorts the terrorist hijacker to a secure area of the airplane. Kim saunters up to Joe, and holds him with her trembling arms.

Finally, the airplane lands in England. Joe, holding his parrot Herbie, exits the aircraft and walks to the front of the airport. He attempts to wave down a taxi with no luck. Herbie whistles loud. A taxi stops in its tracks, burning off tire rubber. *Skid!* "You Yanks need a lift?" the taximan says.

Joe and Herbie get inside. "Buckingham Palace, please," Joe says.

They arrive at Buckingham Palace. Joe gives the taxi driver several pounds, while Herbie gives him one shilling. "Gee, thanks," the driver says.

Joe pulls out his royal cell phone, dials a number, and says, "I'm here, sire."

"Outstanding! Ready for the Game of Kings?" the king says.

The palace guards escort Joe to the grounds, where the king's team is losing in a fiercely played polo match. "You bloody well better get in here, Joe!" the king commands.

As Joe walks, he has an uneasy feeling, and then he's suddenly hugged from behind. "I love you!" Charlotte says. Joe is ecstatic, but he wonders how his fiancée was able to sneak up on him. He is, after all, a samurai warrior.

Herbie shakes his parrot head and says, "Love Joe. Love … awk!"

Joe suits up and saddles up as, sensing that his polo pony has become ecstatically inspired by his rider's presence. Joe places his left hand on the pony's neck and strokes it to calm the pony's anxiety. He says, "Let's have some fun, pony!" Joe sees the king lose the wooden polo ball to the opponents, so instantly he charges, and intercepts the wooden ball. Joe focuses with Zen-like precision. Then he swings his long-handled mallet, its head striking the ball to score, tying the match.

The king and Joe form an admirable team. An opponent named Brutus charges Joe, swinging his whip at Joe's face. But Joe, leveraging his neck muscles, moves out of harm's way, and avoids being struck in the face. But the whip strikes Joe's pony in the face. The pony runs wild briefly, but Joe quickly regains control.

Charlotte, looking on, worriedly cries, "Joe, honey, my love."

Brutus, laughing, and now in control of the wooden ball, sees Joe charging. He swings his whip again toward Joe's face. But this time Joe uses his mouth to catch and clamp onto the whip; consequently, this causes blood to pour profusely from Joe's lips. Then Joe, with Brutus's horsewhip in his mouth, flexes his neck and jaw muscles, and tilts his head right, using leverage. *Boom!* Brutus falls hard to the ground. Charlotte jumps up and down for joy. Joe swings his mallet, striking the ball in the direction of the king for an assist. The king swings his mallet, striking the ball for a game-winning score. "Yes!" the king shouts happily.

The polo game over, Joe and the king sit down to talk about another Halloween approaching. A manservant brings them a cup of joe. Joe senses that the king is nervous, or troubled about some mysterious matters. "Let's *joust* a little, sire. This will help us men think more wisely. What do you think, sire?" Joe says.

The king thinks quickly and says, "Cheers!" Both Joe and the king clasp their cups of coffee and drink down the last of the smooth and bitter-tasting brew. They both adjourn to the gym, and put on fencing gear to joust.

"Now. En garde, Joe!" the king says. Joe closes his eyes, reaches out, and flicks the king's foil out of his hands.

"Incredible! Damn bloody incredible!" the king says.

"I got lucky, sire," Joe says.

"Let's try the sabers, Joe. I want to have eternal peace about sending a future family member on a possible suicide mission," The king says. Then Joe and the king begin clanging their swords hard. Sparks fly from the sabers' blades. Joe senses that the king is a powerful dominant man, a man of honor, and a very efficient swordsman.

As they both continue their swordplay, the king says, "Joe, it's hard being king sometimes. And I am worried for your life, Joe. This mission of Halloween is the most dangerous task I've ever assigned to a royal knight!" Horrendous sparks fly off their swords. The king comes after Joe hard. Suddenly, Joe disarms the king, breaking the king's saber in two. The pieces fall to the floor. *Clunk! Clank!* Then the king mutters, "Joe, why? And how did you break this top-grade steel saber?" The king leers in astonishment.

Joe smiles and says, "It slipped." He happily looks at the king from the corner of his eye.

"You're ready, Joe! You're bloody ready for any mission!" the king jubilantly proclaims.

The two gentlemen chat about possible strategies for the upcoming mission of Halloween. As they walk down a corridor, the king says, "Come, Joe. There is something I want to show you." The corridor narrows. They enter a secret chamber where relics are kept. The king takes a brass skeleton key from his pocket and places it into the keyhole of a chest made of petrified wood. Once he turns the key—*kaboom*—the medium-sized chest pops open. Inside, Joe sees a knight's shining suit of armor. The king says, "Joe, this suit of armor is what was left behind by England's greatest knight, William Marshal." Joe smiles as the king continues. "William Marshal was a master swordsman and a royal knight who won many jousting matches and military campaigns for king and country. His suit of armor is made from a meteorite that fell from the sky, just as William was praying that he would become a royal knight to fight for righteousness, against all evil. The unusual metal that came from this meteorite is a combination of titanium and an unknown substance that makes it very light but very strong. Unfortunately, only the upper portion of William Marshal's suit of armor, which protects the chest, abdomen, and back, was preserved, and kept under lock and key. At first glance, the armor looks as if it is made of copper, but then with another glance, it appears to be made of stainless steel that shines as light strikes it."

Joe, studying the suit of armor, says, "This knight's suit of armor has chameleonlike characteristics, blending in with its surroundings." Joe takes the late, great champion William Marshal's suit of armor out of the box and places it against several different backgrounds, revealing the armor's ability to change colors in order to blend in with the background. After donning the armor, Joe moves left and then right, very fast and unhindered by the suit of armor, which he is now wearing at the king's request. "Wow, amazing!" Joe enthusiastically shouts. The armor is a perfect fit.

The king proudly says, "Yes, Joe! The suit of armor is yours. Take it to battle, when you deem it fit to use a knight's armor for a particular mission you're on. And I recommend you use this armored suit on the very dangerous upcoming mission of Halloween."

CHAPTER 11

Several weeks go by. The king of England, along with his queen, and Charlotte and Joe—the latter of whom has Herbie on his shoulder—greets Rose, who has just arrived in England from Beverly Hills. Joe gives his sister a hug. Herbie kisses Rose on her cheek. Then Rose and Charlotte hug. Rose says to her, "Let's go wedding dress shopping."

Charlotte looks at Joe. "Even though you're far away sometimes, you thought you could escape from us?" she mysteriously says. Joe says his good-byes to everyone, accepting a long kiss and a hug from his fiancée.

Joe then departs Buckingham Palace. He and Herbie get the same taxi driver to take them back to the airport. "You again?" Herbie and the taximan say at the same time.

Joe just laughs as he gets into the taxi. "California, here we come," he says.

Herbie says, "Step on it, chap." This time he tosses two shillings at the taximan, saying, "Awk!"

"Gee, thanks!" the taximan says.

Rose stays at Buckingham Palace to help Charlotte send out invitations and go wedding dress shopping.

Charlotte and Rose get into the royal limousine with a chauffeur, who is also a royal bodyguard. Their limousine drives down

Abbey Road. Ecstatic, they stop at the fabulous Shop Le Tessy, where the famous medium Gilda, who reads palms, is working. At the Shop Le Tessy, Charlotte insists, "Get your palm read, Rose!"

"Why would I want my palm read, Charlotte?" Rose inquires.

"It's fun! Besides, I want to know what Gilda has to say about your future!" Charlotte says. The ladies laugh.

The lovely Gilda begins to read Rose's palm. *"Ahh! Your brother!"* Gilda shouts. She runs out of Shop Le Tessy, screaming at the top of her lungs.

Charlotte says, "Interesting."

"Why did she run out screaming in fear?" Rose wonders.

Suddenly, the owner, Madam Tessy, enters from a hidden door and says, "May I help you, ladies?"

Charlotte enthusiastically conveys her desire to Madam Tessy, saying that she hopes to acquire an exquisite wedding dress.

Charlotte tries on a few wedding dresses. Finally she says, "Rose, this is the one! It's beautiful!"

Madam Tessy says, "I think we need to tailor-fit this dress now." Rose concurs.

The tailor comes in—Lady Fluffy, she is called. Fluffy says, "You'll be fitted and wrapped like a pumpkin, sweetie." Madam Tessy oversees everything as the dress is made ready for the bride to walk down the aisle.

Once Charlotte and Rose exit Shop Le Tessy, a man outside with darkened rings around his eye says, "Hey there, want to have some fun?"

The royal bodyguard pulls out his huge handgun, points it at the man's head, and says, "No, no, no. Get back, chap!" The man retreats in fear. After Charlotte and Rose are safely inside the limousine, the chauffeur speeds away. They arrive at Buckingham

Palace. Charlotte gives her wedding dress to her servant to hide it until her wedding day. Charlotte quietly says, "Rose, I have to see Joe."

"Then let's take the next flight to California!" Rose exclaims.

CHAPTER 12

Joe's flight arrived safely in California. Joe awoke early in the morning, yawning in his bed at Benson Manor. Herbie, soaring around and keeping a watchful eye on his friend Joe, says, "Garden, Joe." Then Herbie flies out to the garden through the open bedroom window.

Joe rises from his comfortable bed, walks over to his altar, drops down on his knees, and starts his prayer, saying, "Our Father who art in heaven, hallowed be thy name; thy kingdom come, thy will be done, on earth as in heaven. Give us this day our daily bread, and forgive us our sins, as we forgive those who sin against us. I love you, God, so please give me strength if or when temptation comes, but please don't lead me into temptation, and do not put me to the test, but deliver me from the Evil One. Amen."

This is the key that permits the archangel Joe to visit heaven. Joe walks in heaven as the spirit archangel of honor. Heaven is glorious, with a brilliant orb of light, which is God's holy presence, surrounding everything. Joe kneels down before God and says, "My holy Father, please give me strength to succeed in this mission of Halloween, for I wish to marry the woman Charlotte and experience life and love of a family." There is a humble quietness.

Then God speaks to Joe. "Joe, your love of Charlotte and your faith in the Lord will lead you to overcome all adversities at this time. I am with you, my son. I love you. Don't worry, Joe!" God says.

Joe wipes away his tears and says, "I love you, God!" Joe then departs, returning to earth changed back into his human form. As he comes out of his prayer, he finds himself on his knees beside his altar.

Joe takes a deep breath, stands up gracefully, and walks over to his calendar to look ahead. "Hmm. Another Halloween night approaching!" he says.

CHAPTER 13

A week before Halloween night, back at the evil witch Samara's castle, the place where the crying Angelina was taken shortly after she had been abducted from the Vatican by the henchmen of Mother Superior Samara, Angelina is stripped naked by Samara's followers, her beautiful curvy body exposed. Angelina is tied with leather straps to a black grindstone. Samara paints a bluish-green dye, made from the mineral jade, all over Angelina's body. Once used by the Maya, this bluish-green jade dye was historically placed on the bodies of designated victims who were to be sacrificed in honor of Satan's birthday on Halloween night.

Samara waves her hand over her crystal ball. It lights up. She looks deeply into it and chants in Latin, *"Meus rex, diabolus!"* (My king, the Devil!) Looking into her crystal ball, she says, "You have promised me that I will become the papa if I dispose of the papa."

Satan says, with an evil beguiling laugh, "You have my word!"

Then Samara waves her hand over the glowing crystal ball. It goes dark. Samara, a little tired, commands, "Japanra! You are my smartest witch. Please hold the Book of Itzamna for safekeeping until the next Halloween night!"

"Yes, Samara! I will guard this Book of Knowledge for safekeeping in Japan!" Japanra says.

CHAPTER 14

Time goes by. It is now a few days before Halloween night. Joe is at home in Beverly Hills, relaxing in the mansion's garden. The sun is shining, birds are chirping, fish are splashing in the brook, and insects are humming and buzzing. Joe is in the seiza posture, his knees on the floor, sitting on the rear of his calves and heels of his feet. Joe has his shirt off while soaking up the sun. He sharpens his holy sword of honor with a special ancient Templar stone. Herbie flies through the air and lands on Joe's shoulder. "Sharpen the sword, Joe! We have a mission tomorrow!" Herbie says.

"We have a mission, Herbie?" Joe says with a slight laugh. Then Joe grabs the soft polishing rag next to him, and starts polishing his sword. A professional gladiator he is. The sword, once it is polished, looks like a clear mirror.

Joe and Herbie can be seen their reflection in the sword. Herbie shouts, "Joe, look! We're a team. Awk!"

"Yes we are!" Joe concurs, observing the remarkable reflection of him and Herbie in the sword.

Joe reflects back in time, remembering his late sensei, Musashi, teaching him *reiho* (etiquette). Joe remembers standing, holding his sword in its scabbard, and bowing to Sensei Musashi. Then Joe lowered himself down on his knees, and placed his sword on the ground in front of him. He bowed to his sword. He remembers Sensei Musashi saying, "Etiquette, Joe, is the first lesson for a martial artist who studies the way. Etiquette will also be your final lesson at the end of your life, your manners determining how people will remember you. Good etiquette will also help you achieve eternal life, Joe."

While Joe is daydreaming, Charlotte walks pretentiously toward him. "Rose told me you were back here," she says. She scans Joe's athletic chest, abdomen, and arms, as Joe, along with Herbie, polishes the magnificent sword.

"I'm glad you're here. You look great, Charlotte!" Joe says.

"Charlotte look great!" Herbie squawks. Charlotte sits down next to her fiancé to caress his body. Then she passionately kisses him. Now Joe and Charlotte hold the same polishing rag, as Joe shows Charlotte how to polish a sword. "Polish the sword, Charlotte … two days … mission! Awk!" Herbie rambles on.

Charlotte inquires, "Mission? Joe, it's a few days until Halloween. What mission, Joe?"

"Yes. The mission is getting a lot of Halloween candy, Charlotte, for you. Let's watch a movie," Joe says, eyeballing Herby as if to scold him for his loose tongue.

"I flew in from London to be with you, Joe. Yes, sweetheart. Let's watch a movie. Besides, Rose came with me. However, she got into some limousine with a very handsome magnate."

Just then Joe receives a text from his sister. "Love you, Joe. I'm with Bubo. Don't worry. Kiss, kiss."

Joe and Charlotte, holding a wooden bowl, begin to eat some popcorn. Herbie puts his parrot feet into the bowl and snags some popcorn. Herbie says, "Butter, Joe? Where's butter?"

"Shh! Quiet, Herbie," Joe says. They all watch a movie called *Enter the Dragon* on the technologically advanced seventy-inch television. Joe and Charlotte observe a concerned facial expression on Bruce Lee's face as he gazes at an island filled with evil-looking characters who are on the shore awaiting the arrival of Lee and his companions.

"Look at his mysterious expression, Joe. What's he thinking?" Charlotte wonders.

"I believe it's his sixth sense alerting him to the evil on that Island," Joe says. He and Charlotte munch on warm popcorn with no butter. As Joe and Charlotte enjoy quality time, with Herbie sipping on a soda, Joe receives a text from the Vatican. It's a blessing from the pope: "Joe, everything is prepared. Godspeed. In the name of the Father, Son, and the Holy Ghost. Amen!"

CHAPTER 15

It's still a few days before Halloween night. Back in the Vatican, the pope takes a drink with a slightly pungent odor offered by the Italian nun Romanra, hoping to quench his thirst. The pope says, "A peculiar taste, but refreshing, child."

Romanra's black pupils burst open, dilating like those of a gray-white shark. She says, "Relax, Papa!"

The pope suddenly has a headache, and goes to lie down on his bed to rest.

A half hour has passed. One of the priests checks in on the papa's health. The priest screams, *"Mama mia!"* as he observes the pope's head swollen like a Halloween pumpkin. The pope is rushed to the Vatican hospital, but mysteriously he does not die of cerebral edema. Although he is very ill, he is healthy enough to speak to the abbess Samara.

Samara walks in. Judging by her facial expression, she seems to be in shock.

"Why, you look as if you've seen a ghost, child," Papa says.

"You're alive?!" Samara cries.

"Yes, but my energy is weakened. I need you to temporarily take charge, Samara. You will temporarily have power. You are the esteemed abbess, and like a daughter to me. … I have ordered this," Papa says.

The pope announces to the world that the abbess Samara will be in charge of all Vatican matters while he recovers from his illness.

Abbess Samara thinks, *Accusator mentiti sunt mihi. Quia tempus non fore potestatem meam.* (The Accuser lied to me. He did not say my power would be temporary power.) Samara sobs.

Then, within hours of the pope's proclamation vesting Abbess Samara's with power, the pope slips into a coma. Soon he dies from a sudden recurrence of cerebral edema. Samara has now received total permanent power! And now she has the title "Mama Papa."

Samara exits her esteemed room gloriously, and goes out onto the balcony, where a huge crowd of people has gathered below. Television cameras rolling, flashbulbs flash furiously. Various news agencies are broadcasting live all across the world. "Mama Papa! Mama Papa! Mama Papa!" they all cheer.

CHAPTER 16

Halloween night has arrived. And unbeknownst to the Mama Papa, the late pope's Halloween mission will continue in secrecy as planned. All royal knights arrive from all over the world at their instructed meeting place, the seaport of San Diego, wearing their shining suits of armor and wielding shields and swords. The leader and strongest of all the royal knights is the human archangel of honor, Joe, with his companion Herbie the parrot. Joe, with Herbie perched on his left shoulder, walks onto the gangway to board the sleek ship named the *Dolphin*, along with his comrade royal knights named McBrian, George, Sanchez, and Buck, among other royal knights. Finally, the men of various religions arrive. They also get aboard the *Dolphin*. With confidence and faith, the pastors, priests, padres, ministers, reverends, deacons, swamis, monks, and so forth anticipate their journey on the *Dolphin*, a bullet-shaped EcoBoat whose figured resembles the face of a dolphin. This is a marine-mammal-inspired passenger boat that runs on hydrogen. It has many seats, with large glass windows so the passengers can view the vast ocean and the stars in the sky while they ride the rough seas. Joe is in the front of the boat. As he prepares to steer at the helm, he hears whispered advice from Herbie: "Say a prayer, Joe. Awk!"

Just before they depart on their Halloween mission, Joe

says, "Everyone, there are forty of us present, so let's all come together!" They all unite as one family, and Joe says a prayer: "Though we journey through darkness, while fearing the shadows of death, I see a light. We do not fear the unknown, for we know you, Lord. Amen!"

Everyone breathes in the fresh ocean air. They all sigh, united in strength, as they begin their journey. Joe starts up the ship's powerful engines. *Varoom!* He pushes a button on the panel, and the ship's anchor is lifted. Then he moves the throttle with his powerful hands. The ship takes off.

It's a beautiful day in sunny San Diego. The seawater splashes up into the air from the bottom of the ship as it darts through large swells of ocean water. Joe, the ship's skipper, steering at the helm, looks left and right. He sees dolphins swimming alongside the ship, which is known as bow riding. Herbie says, "Chirp! We have hitchhikers, Joe."

Joe just smiles as he looks over the pope's scroll, studying the hieroglyphics. "Hmm. I'm grateful that Lumbra taught me how to decipher ancient codes," Joe says, thinking, *Sensei Musashi was right when he instructed me and said, "Joe, a samurai must continue to thirst for knowledge!"* That was one of the best lessons Joe received from his late teacher. As Joe reviews the scroll, he notices it has ancient coded directions to the Gulf of Mexico and the Bermuda Triangle—or, as some call it, Devil's Triangle. They head for the mysterious Halloween Island.

Joe is both leader and skipper of this mission. However, no one is aware that hidden inside the boat is the youngster Wheels. He desperately wants to be a knight like Joe, and find his beautiful Angelina.

Joe says, "Sir George, you used to be in the navy. Come here, please, and take over the sailing duties for a brief moment."

George nonchalantly struts over, pours himself a cup of joe, and then takes the helm from Joe.

"Aye-aye, Skipper! Let a real navy sailor take over!" George says after he receives the latitude and longitude from Joe. Joe laughs appreciatively, and then sits down on the deck with his legs crossed in the lotus position. He slowly closes his eyes to go into a deep meditation. Four royal knights who are near Joe observe him.

Sir George says, "What's Joe doing?"

Sir Sanchez says, "I don't know. Maybe we should sneak up on him to test his awareness. *Que te paracer?*" (What do you think?)

"I don't know, lads. Only a fool or a demon would try to sneak up on Joe. He's our best knight, man. Joe is perfect, and he's our leader, laddies!" Sir McBrian adds.

Sir Buck says, "No one is perfect. Every human has a flaw. Even the so-called beautiful-in-every-way Lucifer with the grand wings of a cherub had a flaw. Lucifer's pride and grand splendor corrupted him into thinking he could be on the throne of the Most High. However, only God is good in every way. Listen, comrades! This is why we work as a team. If we spot a flaw, we step in immediately, even if it cost us our life!"

A few feet away, at the helm, George says, "Quiet, mates! Everything happens for a reason, gentlemen. We fight for the king and for our God!" That concludes the royal knights' conversation.

A short time passes.

Joe slowly opens his eyes from meditation. With rejuvenated energy, he approaches the helm. "I'll take over now, George."

"Thanks, brother." George smiles and walks away to join the other royal knights.

Suddenly, a beautiful siren's enchanting song is heard through the sea air. Her soft voice sings, *"Amirah! Amirah!"* It seems to calm the men as it lures them. *"Amirah! Amirah!"*

Joe, very concerned, quickly says, "Cover your ears—now, men!"

The siren suddenly changes her soft voice to a scream. She makes a loud, spooky, squeaky sound.

"Augh! Augh!" One of the royal knights' ears burst open—*pop!* His ears bleed profusely. He loses his equilibrium and falls overboard. The siren then quickly grabs him, controlling his defensive actions, and whisks him away underwater.

Herbie suggests, "Joe, must go ahead! No stop. Awk!" Joe, sighing deeply, looks up to the stars to continue navigating. He agrees that the mission must go on. The powerful *Dolphin* moves forward.

The Irish priest looks through his binoculars to scan the sea. From afar, he watches in fear as the siren hungrily eats the flesh of the royal knight on a rock that is slightly above sea level. He says, "Aye, son ... mercy, laddie." The Irish priest grieves. Then mysteriously, while former seaman George monitors the ship's gauges for latitude and longitude, the gauges go haywire as the *Dolphin* moves through the Devil's Triangle. Joe, not worried, looks through his wide-lens sextant to continue navigating as the ship proceeds forward.

Instantly, a ferocious storm of rain with skin-cutting wind hits those aboard in the face. Cold seawater splashes over them all, causing them to shake and shiver. The boat rocks back and forth on the waves, occasionally sinking deep into the swells. A few of the religious men fall overboard and drown. "We will all be lost at sea!" many men shout.

Joe remembers being taught many military skills and celestial navigation by his late grandfather General Benson, who was in the Army Rangers and later in the Special Forces Green Beret Unit. Grateful for his training, Joe says, "Don't worry!" He looks for the star Polaris, often called the North Star. Quickly spotting it, he steers the helm accordingly, moving in the direction of what the scroll indicates is Halloween Island.

The royal knights shout, "We will succeed!"

The religious men shout, "We have faith, Father!" Joe gleams with pride in his great team.

A short while later, with the full moon shining, the boat approaches the area where Halloween Island should be. Joe looks high up into the air and sees a huge bird called the *Argentavis magnificens* with a wingspan of seven meters. And has on its back is a woman rider, wearing a black dress with black boots while her long black hair is seen flapping in the wind. "What? No way!" Joe says.

"Witch, Joe. Awk!" Herbie says. Then suddenly a brown horned owl perches on the ship's bow, its huge glowing eyes watching them. "Spy, Joe! Big-eyed bird spy, Joe! Awk!" Herbie warns.

Joe says, "Someone knows we're here, men. However, our contract is to retrieve information from Namas and learn of Halloween's mystery. Hopefully we can still make contact with this Namas."

The boat continues forward. Herbie trots toward the horned owl, which flies off into the sky. Then, the designated scribe begins to write in the ship's logbook, while Joe says a prayer: "God almighty, please record on this Halloween night that brave men came here, putting their lives on the line, not knowing if we would be successful, but we, in this fight of good versus evil, will try to succeed, in the name of the Lord! Amen!"

Just as Joe concludes, Sir Buck uses his huge hand to tap lightly on Joe's back. "I'll be at your side, mate—the bloody whole time, Joe. So get used to it, friend!" Buck consoles.

"Thanks, Buck," Joe says, reassured.

As the strong sea currents attempt to control the ship unsuccessfully, Joe steers the helm off the Gulf of Mexico inside the Devil's Triangle. Hauntingly, on this Halloween night, an island suddenly mysteriously appears on the horizon before their eyes.

"Wow! Where did that bloody island come from, mate?" Sir George slurs.

Joe says, "Gentlemen, behold, that's Halloween Island!"

Because of the magnificently rough sea current, the boat becomes stuck on a reef and falls twenty feet short of reaching this mysterious Island of Halloween. The men of the cloth, becoming nervous, start praying.

Sir McBrian says, "Not to worry, gentlemen. Aye, like they say back in old Ireland, it takes an Irishman to do the hard task!" McBrian jumps off the boat. *Splash!* He walks his huge powerful Irish body to shore, carrying the boat's anchor and chain. McBrian's huge six-foot-ten-inch frame of massive muscle pulls the ship, which glides along the water to shore. *Whoosh!*

"Hooray for McBrian!" everyone cheers. Then the bird of doom, an albatross, lands next to a horned owl that is perched in a tree. The horned owl says, *"Whoo, whoo!"* A bit later, the men hear, *"Rrrr! Rrrr!"* It is the big-eyed horned owl growling like a bobcat. Then the owl quickly flies off toward the huge hill in the center of the island.

Joe gives the order for two royal knights, Peters and Ross, to stay back to guard the ship. They comply, saying, "Yes sir, Joe." Joe then quickly unsheathes his archangel holy sword. *Swift!* Then, following Joe's lead, the other royal knights unsheathe their royal swords. *Swift! Swift!* All royal knights are master swordsmen. They have their swords at the ready, prepared for this dangerous mission of Halloween.

As everyone begins to debark the ship, three huge red snakes appear from out of nowhere, slithering and hissing, and spitting out fire as they come closer to Joe and his crew. Calmly, Joe looks up to the heavens and says, "Father!" He gently lays his holy sword on the ground, where it suddenly turns into a giant white snake. The white snake fights furiously with the three red snakes, and then devours them. *Slurp! Slurp! Slurp!* Slowly, the white snake metamorphoses back into the holy sword. "Thank you, Lord!" Joe picks up his sword, looks at his map, and says, "Let's head in the direction of the firelight at the top of the hill, gentlemen! Let's go, royal knights! Head 'em up; move 'em out!" Joe commands.

Herbie, sitting on Joe's left shoulder, says, "Move it! Move it! Move it!" The royal knights assume a protective triangular marching battle formation. Some knights have armored shields. Joe is out in front, leading them. The men of the cloth follow close behind.

After a thousand meters of walking, Joe softly says, "My sixth sense feels danger. It seems we should stop. However, we must push forward, men. We are on a mission!"

"Don't worry, Joe. Awk!" Herbie consoles. Joe eats sunflower seeds and gives some to Herbie. *Crunch!* Grunting and groaning through the thick brush, some of the holy men stumble to the ground. However, with strong faith and tolerance, they get up and continue walking. Fat mouse-sized spiders try climbing up their legs. They all squat down at various times, tap their heads, and count off to conduct a head count, as instructed by Joe. Then they stand up and continue walking.

The men hear a lion growling, seemingly hungry. *Growl! Growl!* Although they never see the lion, they know it's some kind of beast following them. They are about to go into a dark area, so Joe stops and reviews his map, studying the ridges and valleys. He opens up his grandfather's military compass. He motions with his hand for the others to follow him. They enter a dark abyss in columns of two. A short while later, they exit the dark abyss, still in columns of two. Then they squat and do a head count. Those present discover that there are two missing—one priest and one royal knight. Joe is saddened, but he and the remaining men must move on and reach the designated encounter point before midnight.

They all finally approach an open area, frightened to see what look to be Aztec and Mayan warriors standing all along the perimeter of a pyramid made of crystal. These warriors mysteriously show no emotion whatsoever. At the top of the elegant crystal pyramid is a scantily clothed muscular man with his entire face painted turquoise. On his head is a chief's headdress. This man has the commanding presence of a leader. Joe shouts up to this man, "Who is Namas? We need to speak to Namas! Please."

The large man atop says rhetorically, "Namas?" He is fierce-looking, with a bellowing voice that echoes. Then suddenly, this leader begins to shake his face and body, screaming in a high pitch, *"Rrrrr! Aaaa! Eeee!"*

Simultaneously all Aztec and Maya warriors below shake, screaming, *"Rrrrr! Aaaa! Eeee!"* Parts of their faces and bodies fall off like clay pieces, revealing horrific-looking demon devils.

Battle-ready, Joe and the royal knights have their swords out. Joe instructs, "Shields up!" With faith, two priests, two padres, two ministers, two reverends, two rabbis, two deacons, two pastors, two monks, and two imams walk in front of the royal knights. They are all reading their holy books, whether the Book of Mormon, the Quran, or the New Testament or the Old Testament of the Holy Bible. These holy men pair up—one of each pair holding the holy book, and the other holding a cross, a bell, incense, or some other religious item. Joe grasps his archangel holy sword firmly in both hands. All the royal knights have their swords drawn out in front of their bodies.

The Irish priest, taking the lead, bravely says to the demons, "Repent and change! It is the only way earth will finally have peace eternal!" The men of the cloth pray out loud.

Moved by the priest's speech, the big demon atop the pyramid raises up his powerful arms. Wielding what appears to be a sharp knife, he says, "I am Saman!" The men of the cloth, who are united, do not fear the big man's knife.

This is the mission of Halloween! Convincing evil people to change and return to God so that the many will benefit is the most important thing!

It looks as if one of the demons closest to the Irish priest is crying.

The crying demon motions for the big Irish priest to come closer toward him. *A gesture of good faith?* Thinks the Irish priest. Feeling empathy, he moves forward by himself, coming close to the hideous demon, until the two are face-to-face. The priest says, "Yes, brother! We can do this! Somebody here has to make the first move. I do not fear you, for this mission of Halloween will always be remembered." The proud priest's eyes reflect his courage and divine faith.

Another Catholic priest says, "Be careful!" Nevertheless, the proud Irish priest opens up his Holy Bible to read a passage, still standing alone, face-to-face with the hideous demon. The demon's facial expression is one of friendship as he reaches forward with his scaly fungus-smelling hand, moving it slowly toward the Irish priest. Then he violently plunges his demonic hand deep into the Irish priest's chest—*kerplunk!*—and pulls out the priest's beating heart. *Lub-dub, lub-dub,* the priest's heart sounds loudly, as the eyes on his face lock wide open. Shocked silence is in the atmosphere. No one moves. The Irish priest falls hard to the ground—*thud!*

Suddenly, a woman screams from atop the pyramid—*"Aaaa!"*—breaking the moment of silence.

Joe looks and sees a lovely girl who appears to be about sixteen years old. She is bound, her naked body covered with blue dye, at the altar atop the pyramid.

Ferocious fighting breaks out everywhere around the pyramid at ground level. Because of their courage, many of the men of the various religious faiths refuse to run. Rather, they hold their holy books and pray, as they are violently slaughtered by demons.

A pastor of the Seventh - day Adventist faith, who is an athlete, runs toward the top of the pyramid, toward the young girl, with his huge Bible held out in front of his body and shouting, "No! In the name of Jesus!" The royal knights do their best fighting, along with the archangel Joe, but there are too many demons on this Halloween night, on Halloween Island, to overcome. Many religious men and several royal knights are killed.

The demons shout upward, in the direction of the huge muscular demon atop the pyramid altar, "Saman! Saman!" Saman is now wearing a mysterious jade mask, with his large ugly yellowish-fungus-covered teeth protruding from it. Joe runs up the pyramid steps toward the sacrificial altar, ferociously swinging his sword downward and horizontally, slicing demons in half while continuing forward, lopping off arms and two or three demon heads with one graceful swing of his holy sword. Then, unfortunately, Joe gets sliced in his back with a devil's claw. *"Augh!"* Yet he perseveres, making his way through demons with tolerance. He finally makes his way to the top of the pyramid steps, as does the Seventh - day Adventist pastor, miraculously.

Joe sees the demon called Saman holding his big sacrificial

knife over the young girl's beating chest, which is going up and down with fear. She screams again: *"Aaaa!"*

The pastor reaches the girl and says, "Do not worry, child." Saman places his strong left hand on the pastor's neck, squeezing it, choking the pastor, but the pastor does not care, because he is buying time for Joe to rescue the young girl. Saman plunges his knife deep into the pastor's chest. *"Augh! It is finished,"* the pastor cries, cradling the Bible. Those are his last words.

Joe continues fighting demons, as more and more of them, coming from inside the pyramid, rush him, attempting to stop him from interfering with the sacrifice of the virgin girl. He gets help from the huge royal knight McBrian, who comes to his aid. McBrian, holding his large armored shield out in front of his body, pushes demons out of Joe's way with his powerful muscles. Demons fall off the pyramid. *Kerplunk! Bam! Thump!* He clears the path quickly for Joe. In the meantime, Sir Buck arrives to aid them. But more demons suddenly appear. Joe's adrenalin kicks in more, since he's an accomplished, experienced, courageous warrior. The human archangel Joe, knight of honor, does a smooth slide step forward and powerfully side-kicks a demon off the pyramid. *Thump!* The demon falls atop the demons below.

Then, tragically, the royal knight McBrian is speared in his back with a sword held by one of the fallen angel fighters, the demon called Molech. *"Augh!"* Sir McBrian cries in pain. Molech pushes McBrian's injured body down the pyramid steps to his death. *Kaboom!* Then Molech runs away, disappearing. Joe and Buck are enraged by their comrade's death. They are followed by royal knights George and Sanchez.

Atop the pyramid, Joe gets burned by a sudden fire demon wall, formed to shield Saman from Joe. But Joe doesn't care. He goes into a trance, using his mind just as the ancients did when they walked barefoot across fiery lava without getting burnt. Joe jumps through the wall of fire. His royal knight uniform repels the fire, forming a sphere of fire protection around him.

Four large demons with razor-sharp swords attack Joe from the front with slashes and stabs. Joe gallantly deflects their swords with his powerful sword. *Clank! Clank!* However, from Joe's rear, the powerful beguiling demons Beelzebub and Hades, using their powerful demonic swords, violently attack Joe with horizontal slashes and thrusting stabs to his back. *Clunk! Clank!* They strike ferociously at Joe's suit of armor. *Kalpak! Clank!* Miraculously for Joe, Beelzebub's and Hades's swords chip and crack into pieces while striking him. Their demonic blades do not penetrate Joe's special royal suit of armor.

All the demons growl: *"Guruh!"* Nevertheless, they continue attacking Joe. Joe, taking a breath and using smooth footwork, swings his sword horizontally and lops off four demons' heads. *Kaplan!* Beelzebub and Hades try to push Joe off the pyramid, but they are unsuccessful.

All this time, Wheels had been climbing the back side of the pyramid carefully, without being noticed. "Oh," Wheels says, sighing as he tiredly reaches the top. Then Wheels sees his lovely young Angelina, looking at him with love in her eyes.

Angelina says, "Please, Wheels, help me, love!" Angelina cries before Wheels's eyes. Out of desperation, fighting for her life, she gets one hand free and pulls the jade mask off Saman's face, revealing a skull face with deep saucer eyes, and devil's horns on the top of his head.

"No! My Angelina!" Wheels shouts. He struggles with Saman. Wheels is a wiry, slippery, evasive person; Saman cannot get a good hold on him. Wheels climbs Saman's back like a spider and bites deep into Saman's neck, tearing out a piece of meat the size of a golf ball.

"Augh!" Saman cries in pain, while demonic blood spurts

profusely from his neck. But Saman is too strong. He pushes Wheels away. *Poof!* Wheels almost falls off the pyramid. For dear life, he holds onto the edge at the top of the pyramid. Panicking, Wheels cries. He experiences an enormous adrenaline rush when he helplessly spots his lovely Angelina struggling with Saman. Saman firmly holds his sacrificial knife. There seems to be a quiet frightened pause in the air when Saman growls with delight and raises his muscular arms, the deadly sacrificial knife clutched in his hand. Then he strikes deep into the heart of the young Angelina: *kerplunk!*

"*Aaaa!*" Angelina screams in a loud high-pitched voice that could break glass.

Then, the demon Saman proudly and gently raises his knife, which is dripping with Angelina's blood, up in the air. He shouts loudly, "*Happy birthday, Satan!*" Saman's eyes gleam evilly on this Halloween night. Joe feels helpless, having witnessed the horrible act of young Angelina being sacrificed—and most likely killed. Tears pour from Joe's eyes as he sobs.

Just then, Herbie flies in from a tree and lands on Joe's left shoulder. Herbie says, "God loves you, Joe. Awk!" Joe takes a deep breath to calm himself. Feeling the Holy Ghost at his side, Joe courageously continues fighting demons with his sword. Hades tosses his damaged sword to the ground and picks up a spear. Beelzebub continues to use his damaged sword. Joe intercepts Beelzebub's thrusting sword attack by using a fencing-beat parry defense, his holy sword deflecting his opponent's blade. Then Joe counters with a riposte, smoothly striking his sword downward, cutting Beelzebub in half, killing the demon. *Flop! Flop!* Beelzebub's two body halves fall to the ground. The demon Hades, furious, tries to kill Joe with a long spear that he thrusts at Joe's heart. Joe sidesteps to his left, avoiding the lethal spear, and swings his holy sword right, cutting off Hades's legs. The legs flop on the ground like a lizard's severed tail, still moving. Hades walks on his hands, coming in to bite Joe with his devil teeth. *"Barah!"* Hades screams as he opens his alligator mouth full of teeth. Joe then drops to one knee, waiting on Hades to close the gap.

"Good!" Joe says, powerfully thrusting his divine sword into Hades's heart, killing him with the power of his holy archangel sword.

"Augh!" Hades cried before dropping dead. Green fungus with worms and white pus exit his demon mouth.

Meanwhile, Wheels, unnoticed by Saman, sobs quietly as he unties his bleeding Angelina, who lies motionless on the sacrificial altar. Wheels, relying on his God-given agility and strength, uses his hands and springy feet to get back to the top of the pyramid. Wheels has acquired stealth by walking in churches his whole life, but Wheels's sobbing gets Saman's attention. Saman strikes with his deadly sharp knife, which has Angelina's blood on it, grazing Wheels's face. *"Augh!"* Wheels screams.

Joe arrives and, with his holy sword, intercepts Saman's second piercing strike at Wheels, knocking Saman's knife to the floor. Blood from the knife splats. *Plap!* The battle begins between Joe and Saman. The sadistically mad Saman says, "You fool, how you dare you come here as we honor Satan's birthday on Halloween night?"

Quickly Joe says, "Shut up! I rebuke you! I come here representing good humans, and the Almighty God!" Then Joe cuts off one of Saman's arms.

Saman screams, "Molech! Help me!"

Joe, shocked, looks at the defiled Angelina. Wheels is applying direct pressure to the wound in Angelina's young chest, trying to stop the bleeding. Sir Buck arrives at Joe's side. Joe says,

"Buck! Escort Wheels with the young girl to the boat! And use the medical kit in the boat. Now!"

Buck, who, having once been a physician, has a medical background, nods his head yes. As Buck escorts the young couple back to the ship, he finds it very difficult to keep up with the speedy Wheels, who is sobbing as he carries his Angelina.

Joe's sixth sense runs at full throttle. He turns around and discovers a demon sneaking up on him, as if to blindside him with a surprise attack, for an easy, cowardly kill. Joe, prepared for sneak attacks, is suddenly violently assaulted by the sneaky demon Molech, who is one of the fiercest of Satan's fallen angels. Joe flicks his sword left and spins to his left, using graceful footwork, to intercept Molech's sword. *Clank!* Joe and Molech continue with their deadly swordplay. Satan appears in the background, unbeknownst to Joe. The powerful Satan appears as the feathered serpent, wielding his sword on the sacrificial altar. Molech, from a bucket of dead souls, tosses the ashes of dead human beings at Joe, and then swings his sword downward with blinding speed. A piece of Joe's left ear gets cut off. Joe draws upon his champion's courage to masterfully sword-fight the demonic celestial Molech. Two of Joe's comrades, the royal knights George and Sanchez, wielding their swords, arrive to aide Joe in this fierce battle. They were at the rear assisting the unfortunate holy men of cloth who were slaughtered like lambs. But now they have come to join the fight against the strong demon Molech.

Joe swiftly slashes his sword forward horizontally with his right strong hand, as his right hand spins around his back to transfer his sword to his left hand, to slash forward horizontally again, for a deceptive double attack that grazes Molech's abdomen. *"Ahrr!"* Molech evilly screams, backpedaling away from

Joe's master swordsmanship with his powerful sword. Joe can use his left hand just as well as his right hand in sword play.

Satan, as the feathered serpent, somewhere in the near distance, not joining the fight just yet, has a somewhat posttraumatic stress disorder moment. His mind drifts off, remembering a huge swordfight in heaven where he shouted, *"Don't fight me, Michael! Join me!"* Soon, the feathered serpent's memory fades back to the present. He lies in wait out of Joe's sight, hiding and ready to kill the human Joe.

Joe's sixth sense kicks in. He feels something else in the area but cannot see it, so he remains in the fencing en garde position as he makes several sword thrusts and slashes at Molech.

From a distance, Joe sees Herbie up in the air nodding his head, a sign for Joe to return to the ship. Joe trusts Herbie's advice. He uses his eyes and his body language, gazing into the eyes of his comrades, the royal knights George and Sanchez, for approval to leave. They both nod their heads, indicating that it is okay for Joe to leave. Joe sees Molech backpedaling, no longer fighting hard. Confident, Joe leaves the fight for the two royal knights to finish up. Sir George says, "Don't worry, Joe! We've got this now!"

Sir Sanchez concurs. *"Sí! Tenemos este, compadre!"* Royal knights Sanchez and George are terrific fighters and master swordsmen.

Satan beguilingly waits for Joe to depart the area. Then he sneaks in to help Molech, thrusting his demonic sword into Sanchez's back—*kaplunk!* Sir Sanchez drops gently to the ground. Seeing a vision, he says, "Sí, Dios. Te amo!" (Yes God. I love you!)

George, with a champion's will to win, continues on, a fierce sword battle against him developing with Satan assisting Molech. George says, "You'll never bloody have my soul! I fight for God! And God save the king of England!"

Joe hears a deathly shriek in the distance: *"Nooo!"* It is the voice of his friend, the royal knight George. Joe feels guilty about leaving his fellow royal knights behind, so he says a prayer: "May God bless their last hours."

Herbie flies ahead to the ship. As Joe trots back in the direction of the *Dolphin*, he observes a priest along the way who, staggering, seems traumatized and disoriented. Joe flexes his muscles, picks up the holy man, and flings him over his shoulder. *"Oomph!"* says the priest. Joe carries him off to safety.

Joe arrives at the *Dolphin*, where Herbie and the royal knights Buck, Peters, and Ross are standing guard. Also awaiting Joe is the saddened young man Wheels with his sweetheart, the bloodied Angelina. The holy man gets into the boat and says, "They will never believe me if I tell the truth of what I saw on Halloween night!"

Joe looks at Angelina, and then at Buck, who is holding the medical kit. Buck grievingly says, "No, Joe. I tried my best. I was a doctor once. I'm sorry, but she's expired!" On his knees, Buck sobs, as does Wheels, who is stretched out with his face against the beach, striking the sand with his hands while crying his heart out.

"My Angelina!" Wheels sobs so much that he loses his voice. Fluids spew out from his eyes and mouth. Joe scans the area, and observes owl feathers and parrot feathers all over the place. Then he finally spots a big-eyed horned owl with a broken neck lying on the ground next to the ship. Joe looks at Herbie.

Herbie says, "He drew first blood, Joe! Awk!" Then courageous Herbie jumps on Joe's left shoulder, and kisses Joe with his little black parrot tongue to comfort him.

Joe, with empathy, double checks the sixteen-year-old Angelina's vital signs, finding no pulse and no heartbeat. Joe, shedding an enormous amount of tears, cries out, "Lord, why must the young suffer when they have their whole lives ahead of them?" He then places a blanket over Angelina's lovely face and naked body, which is still covered with jade paint. Then he gently takes her innocent dead body aboard the *Dolphin*, saying softly, "Rest here. God has not forsaken thee, princess. We will leave soon!"

Joe, continuing to sob, lets his guard down while waiting for Sir Sanchez and Sir George to arrive—safe, hopefully. Nearby, however, mysteriously holding a venom-dipped spear and lurking in the shadows, is the feathered serpent, Satan himself. Satan quickly throws his venom-dipped spear from hell toward Joe's heart. Lax and grief-stricken, Joe has his guard down. Buck, alert, jumps quickly in front of Joe, taking Satan's spear deep into his heart. *Kapoof!* "Auh!" Buck shrieks in pain, startling Joe from his temporary disillusionment.

"Buck!" Joe shouts, rushing over to his dying friend. Once Joe reaches Buck, he takes him up in his arms.

The frustrated feathered serpent, in the distance, becomes enraged. "No! No! Why did you save Joe again?" Satan disappointedly screams as he looks up toward heaven, seeking answers.

Joe, sobbing hard, looks at his friend Buck, seeking a reason for his imminent death. Buck mumbles, "Don't worry, Joe! Everything happens for a reason!" Then Buck's eyes begin to flicker. Soon they stop moving. He dies with his eyes wide open.

Joe, taking a deep breath, uses his fingers to close Buck's eyelids. "Rest easy, old friend," Joe says. Then Joe looks at the sobbing Wheels, and makes a command decision. "We will leave now! Mission abort!" Joe says. Everybody climbs aboard the *Dolphin*. Joe, along with Sir Peters and Sir Ross, places Buck's dead body onto the ship. Joe then uses the spear he had taken off his dead friend Buck, and pushes the boat off the sand and into the deep ocean water.

Herbie observes the saddened Joe and says, "The spear, Joe. Throw away. ... Irk!" Joe, with all his strength, throws the demonic spear high up into the air toward the jungle. It miraculously falls downward to strike Satan's left foot, piercing through his foot and into the ground.

"Augh!" Satan evilly screams.

Herbie smiles and says, "Straight ahead, Joe! Awk!" Joe nods his head in approval, steering the helm. He continues to sob, deep and hard, on this Halloween night.

CHAPTER 17

It's Joe and Charlotte's wedding day, which also happens to be Thanksgiving Day. They are at a Catholic church in sunny Beverly Hills, California. The king and queen of England are there, along with the paparazzi and a huge news media presence. Many royal knights are there in full battle dress, their swords at the ready. Joe glances at all of the royal knights. He looks for Sir Sanchez and Sir George but does not see them. The king looks at Joe, then shakes his head to indicate that Sanchez and George did not make it back safely on Halloween night. Joe, a sad expression of guilt instantly crossing his face, wonders why good men have to die.

Napoleon, who is Joe's past Olympic fencing teacher, is also Joe's best man. While Napoleon is standing next to Joe, he senses that something is bothering him. He taps Joe on the shoulder to reassure him that everything happens for a reason.

Lumbra is the maid of honor, and she looks very lovely. "Enough for Napoleon to marry her again," Napoleon says, expressing his thoughts out loud as he watches his wife closely with love in his eyes.

Herbie's beak and feet are clean and shiny, and his feathers are smelling good.

The priest looks at Joe's missing left ear and says, "Hmm."

The wound is a reminder to Joe of the battle between good and evil that took place Halloween night on Halloween Island. Joe has covered the gruesome area where his left ear used to be with his hair, so that Charlotte, and everyone else, will be unable to see the deformed site.

The priest proclaims, "Wherever there is good, there is evil! And wherever there is evil, there is good! There is never one without the other on earth."

Suddenly, a man, a powerful magnate wearing a Water Mason ring, walks in, smiling while looking in the direction of the piano. He sits down a few feet away from the piano. Peacefully and harmoniously, the piano music begins. Everyone can hear the beautiful voice of a young woman singing "Ave Maria." Everyone turns their attention away from Joe and Rose to look in the music's direction. There they see Rose, a renowned pianist, playing the keyboard, her gift to her brother, Joe, and her soon-to-be sister-in-law, Charlotte.

Charlotte, with impeccable timing, enters the church, smiling as her father escorts her to the altar. Upon reaching the altar, Charlotte, noticing that Joe has covered his left ear with his hair, moves his hair back, exposing his injury. After all, her fiancé is a royal knight, a man. Charlotte says, "You are a royal knight, one of God's soldiers, my man! Joe, the man inside you is who I love. I will always love you while you live!" Charlotte smiles, as does Joe.

Herbie, initially at a loss for words, says quietly, "Awk! You the man, Joe!"

After a short and memorable pause, Napoleon opens the box containing the bride's wedding ring. The ring is gorgeous. It looks like Napoleon made it out of a specially designed dried French roll with gold coloring. Joe laughingly says, "Is it food or a ring, Chef Napoleon?"

"Joe, it's a ring, of course, an ancient pure gold ring that Lumbra and I discovered in the pyramids of Mexico, where the Aztecs played the Game of the Gods! So beautiful. ... Enjoy!" Napoleon says. He slaps his free cupped hand over his puckered mouth to make a light popping sound.

Joe, slowly and lovingly, places the ring on Charlotte's finger, as instructed by the priest. Charlotte blushes as her tears flow. The ring is made of rich hand-engraved gold with seven layered rubies, seven layered pearls, and seven surrounding diamonds, with a huge blue diamond in the middle. It is an exquisite priceless artifact.

The priest proudly says, "I now pronounce you man and wife! You may now, Joe, kiss your lovely bride, Charlotte." Joe's eyes gleam with love as he caresses Charlotte and passionately kisses her—now his beautiful wife—on their memorable wedding day. Rose, Joe's loving sister, her eyes flowing with tears upon witnessing this precious moment, plays on a spectacular grand piano and sings one of Joe's favorite songs. "La-la, hmm, la, la-lee."

Everyone is crying and smiling as Napoleon, Lumbra, Herbie, the king of England, his queen, and all the royal knights cheer: "Hurray for Joe and Charlotte!" The priest smiles as a graceful, beautiful white dove flies in suddenly, and alights on the priest's dais. Joe continues kissing his bride, holding her tight, intending to remember this joyful moment. Amen.

About the Author

John Teofilo Padilla Jr. was born in Albuquerque, New Mexico. He is a college graduate from Ottawa University in Liberal Arts. He enjoys plotting courses for new travels. He is a former United States Army Airborne Commando who was awarded the Meritorious Service Medal for chivalry. A retired California Correctional Peace  Officer, John has studied martial arts and fencing, the details of which he integrates into his writing. He currently lives in San Diego, California.

CPSIA information can be obtained
at www.ICGtesting.com
Printed in the USA
FFOW02n0909151217
44098506-43377FF